Agustín Fernández Paz
CORRIDORS
OF SHADOW

Published in 2016 by
SMALL STATIONS PRESS
20 Dimitar Manov Street, 1408 Sofia, Bulgaria
You can order books and contact the publisher at
www.smallstations.com

This book was first published in the Galician language as *Corredores de sombra* by Edicións Xerais de Galicia (Vigo, 2006). The series GALICIAN WAVE: The Way of Fiction exists to showcase the best of Galician young adult fiction in English. More information can be found at www.smallstations.com/wave. More information about Agustín Fernández Paz can be found at www. agustinfernandezpaz.gal.

There are quotations in this book from the following publications: José Ángel Valente, *Landscape with Yellow Birds*, translated by Thomas Christensen (Archipelago Books, 2013); Wisława Szymborska, *Poems New and Collected 1957-1997*, translated by Stanisław Barańczak and Clare Cavanagh (Harcourt Inc., 2000); James Joyce, *A Portrait of the Artist as a Young Man* (B. W. Huebsch, 1916).

This work received a grant from the General Secretariat of Culture of the Ministry of Culture, Education and University Planning of the Xunta de Galicia in the call for translation grants of the year 2015.

Esta obra recibiu unha axuda da Secretaría Xeral de Cultura da Consellería de Cultura, Educación e Ordenación Universitaria da Xunta de Galicia na convocatoria de axudas para a tradución do ano 2015.

ISBN 978-954-384-050-2

Agustín Fernández Paz

Corridors of Shadow

Translated from Galician by **Jonathan Dunne**

 Small Stations Press

for my daughter, Mariña

Memory opens for us light
corridors of shadow.

José Ángel Valente, *Fragments from a Future Book*

I

The time has come, I shan't put if off any longer. I never thought I would end up fulfilling my uncle Carlos' wish, I never imagined I would be capable of smashing the invisible barrier which prevented me from writing down all that happened in the summer of 1995. A summer which is more and more removed in time and in my memory, I was still quite young, and now I see I'm nearing the milestone of thirty. I suppose I needed all this time to acquire a certain distance, for the facts to gain solidity in my mind and to shed their more disturbing aspects. It's been more than ten years, the necessary period to be able to confront this moment when, with fear and trepidation, I undertake this journey to the past, guided only by my words.

Perhaps all I'm trying to do is settle scores, or break with the family ghosts, as Carlos kept asking me. Perhaps these are the reasons which motivate me, any other justification is unnecessary. And yet I'm aware I've also been influenced by news which might appear to have nothing to do with me. When I read in the newspapers, as I've been doing repeatedly over the last few weeks, the effort people have been putting into locating the resting-places of their loved ones, abandoned in anonymous graves after the Spanish Civil War; when I witness their deep desire to recover their remains and rescue them from the abyss of oblivion which devoured them after they were murdered; when I see so many people demanding the opening of common graves from a war which seems so distant, so much part of the twentieth century, but which is still so alive, I feel I cannot remain indifferent.

And then I also experience an urgent need to relate how, albeit involuntarily, I contributed to opening up a grave which everyone wanted to stay closed. It's time to record here the memory of that dead man who could have remained forgotten until the end of the world, were it not for chance, that strange chance which directs our lives and caused me to be in the exact location that morning in July 1995. Even we, the descendants of the victors in the Civil War, can contribute a grain of sand to the collective memory, while others who emerged victorious get on comfortably with lives built on the crime and theft committed during those years. A traitor, a traitor to my class, some would say. They may be right, but that's not how I see it. I cannot change my past, it's true, but nor do I have to let that past end up conditioning the rest of my life.

Memory is powerful, but it's also fragile and tricks us into going where it would like us to. 'Memory opens for us light / corridors of shadow,' wrote José Ángel Valente, a poet I heard Carlos quote so many times he soon became an essential point of reference for me. I'm lucky I still have my diaries from that time, they will be the thread of Theseus which leads me into the labyrinth. They will enable me to reconstruct what happened during those few weeks, they will help me to avoid succumbing to the distortions of memory after so many years. I admit I feel a mixture of shame and tenderness when I read these notebooks which were so important to me during my teenage years. I was just starting to discover life and I used solemn, hackneyed words to describe my feelings, it would take a lot longer for me to master my own language. But I recorded the facts with precision and, if I brush aside the sentimental overlay, the diaries will act as a reliable guide so I can direct my footsteps accurately.

There is a huge distance between me now and the girl I was then, I find it difficult to recognize myself in the words I wrote in the diaries. What I can discern, however, is that this was a period of change. The end of one period and the beginning of another, even though I was scarcely aware of the underground shift taking place within me. I lived it all as an adventure, a breaking of family rules, and didn't notice the seeds of change sprouting inside me, which would direct me towards a new life.

And how not to remember Miguel in this adventure of retracing my footsteps? It was with him I discovered love, the love which can sometimes flood our bodies and illuminate our whole lives. Even if time then proceeded to show me no relationship lasts for ever, except in the novels we invent to hoodwink death, and all have a date of expiry from the very moment they begin.

There was no way of knowing all this back then. I was just a girl of sixteen, with lots of fancy ideas, though I realized there was something inside me which set me apart from the superficiality of most of the other pupils at Santa

María do Mar, the school I attended. A school I remember with fondness, not the hatred others of my generation feel towards theirs. This is something I have to thank my mother for, since, had it been down to my father, I would have gone to Adoradoras or somewhere like that, a school attended by the children of the more established families and the nouveau riche. At my school, however, were all the children of what a sociologist would call Coruña's upper-middle class: liberal families who wanted an education far removed from the shackles of the past and religious obscurantism.

I've barely started and I'm already straying from the point, I have to be more rigorous. Now is not the time to talk about my parents or my life at school. But before I open my diary and get carried away by the events of that sixth of July, I should say something about Soutelo Manor, the place where it all happened.

Soutelo Manor is in the district of Vilarelle and has belonged to my father's family since it was built in the middle of the eighteenth century. The Soutelos have always been the lords of the manor, the nobles who owned most of the land and lived comfortably off the sweat and toil of tenant farmers. A family which was already powerful before the manor was built, linked to some of the major Galician families, such as the Montenegros or the Andrades.

Vilarelle is inland, a far cry from the milder climate of the coast. The town is some thirty miles from Coruña, which is where my parents settled after they were married and where I was born six months later, as some people insisted on reminding me when I was young, though it took me some time to understand what the short distance between these two dates meant.

The manor is situated a little before the town, on top of a hill which slopes down gently to the river. The building has two wings in the shape of an L, but what's really impressive is the walled enclosure which surrounds it, in particular the garden in front of the south façade with its circular fountain and goldfish I liked so much, the orchard stretching as far as the river and, most of all, the wood which began after the allotments behind the building, a wood I loved to roam in when I was a child, it seemed to go on for ever, like the forests in the Grimms' fairy tales I used to read in that beautiful edition Mummy gave me one birthday.

Today I can appreciate the special character and artistic value of the house, but not back then. For me it was always the place where Grandma Rosalía lived, a happy place where I could free myself from the limitations of city life. As long as she was alive, we used to go there often, always for a few days during the holidays and longer in the summer months, when my parents would travel and leave me and my brothers in the care of Grandma and a few maids who treated me like a princess. A privileged treatment I noticed as well in girls from the town's more well-to-do families, who sometimes came to play with me and displayed a submissive attitude towards me which at the time I considered normal.

Grandma Rosalía died in 1993. I'd recently turned fourteen and was less and less interested in spending the holidays in Vilarelle, since life in the city had started to appeal to me. The summer after she died, we went for just a few days and I thought the manor house's time, a time I associated with a childhood I was leaving, was over and done with. What I didn't expect is that, when the family's inheritance was divided, my father would buy Uncle Carlos and Aunt María's shares in the house. He wished to renovate it, he told us when he informed us of his decision, to give it a new lease of life and to have it as a second home. This way he'd avoid the property falling into the hands of anyone who wasn't a Soutelo, a possibility he couldn't accept.

Now, with the distance of years, knowing my father better, I think his reasons were quite different. He may have felt nostalgia for his childhood or have wanted to safeguard the family's property, but more than that was the desire to feel he represented a lineage which, though times had changed, continued to wield influence in the local area. Above the gate, and on the building's main façade, was the family coat of arms, a granite shield, which defied the passing of time. Stone banners and crosses topped by the crowned 'S' of the Soutelos, all symbols of an impressive past, which must have served to confirm to my father a prestige which in the city, though we weren't badly off, was lessened by the power of the traditional families and the large fortunes amassed by those in the construction sector.

As soon as the documents were prepared which made him sole owner of the property, my father undertook repairs to the building. The truth is some parts had deteriorated and others didn't function very well, they belonged to an old way of life, since Grandma Rosalía, after Grandpa died, had not seen fit to modernize anything. So began an intense period of renovations which lasted more than a year and gave the manor house back some of the comfort it had lost through neglect and the passing of time.

In the summer of 1995, the renovations were well underway. In fact all the main wing and the first floor of the side wing, the prettier part, with the veranda I liked so much, were ready to be lived in. All that remained was the ground floor of the side wing, which was formerly used for stables and for storing all sorts of things, and which, after the alterations, would hold a gym and various smaller rooms. In the spring my father decided we would spend the months of July and August in the manor; this way he could keep a close eye on the renovation work and we could breathe new life into the family home.

My mother was pleased by the idea; she planned to devote herself to painting, and the peace and quiet there offered her the ideal conditions. My brothers, the twins, were delighted at the prospect of having free range of the fascinating grounds which surrounded the building. They were also pleased that Daddy had invited our cousins, Aunt María's two children. Although my cousin Alfredo was older than they were – he'd recently turned fourteen – they felt sure he would share their games and adventures, as he had done on previous occasions.

I should have felt the same about my cousin Ana, but the truth is the mere thought of putting up with her made me sick. I suppose it wasn't her fault, she was exactly what you would expect of a seventeen-year-old girl in her social position. She loved to discuss clothes, make-up and boys, topics of conversation I cared little about. I was going through a phase of rebelliousness and self-affirmation, and was drawn to music – Nirvana, the Smashing Pumpkins, and the Clash, the group I most identified with – which was a far cry from the sugary melodies she listened to at all hours.

Which is why I spoke of chance. That summer should have passed by as was expected, those months had been arranged so that we could all enjoy the luxury and pleasures due to us as owners of the manor house: huge rooms, every imaginable comfort, maids to cater to our every whim, days spent in conversation and having fun. But, luckily for me, it wasn't like that. Chance irrupted into my life and changed it so much I was never the same again.

I am well aware a story never has a concrete beginning and starts long before, as is especially the case with the one I'm about to describe. But I have to begin with that sixth of July, going by my diary, because that was the day a skeleton turned up in the side wing, the first skeleton I'd ever seen. How could I suspect this discovery would have such a profound influence on me?

2

I seem to recall the circumstances of that morning very well, though time may have distorted them in my memory. We'd been in the manor for several days and, with the prospect of so many weeks before me, I was trying to find a way to enjoy myself and not to be swept along by boredom. I'd got into the habit every morning of going to a pleasant stone mirador situated at the end of the path which crossed the wood, next to the enclosure wall, which on that side was in fairly poor condition. The mirador or lookout, built entirely from granite aged by the years, appeared to possess the virtue of transporting me to another time. A nearby magnolia tree protected it from the sun, and the honeysuckle growing behind the stone on an old metallic structure gave me the sensation I was somehow isolated from the rest of the world. It was an ideal place to read or to while away the hours, thinking about my things.

That morning, having had the breakfast Celsa prepared for me in the kitchen, I left the house through the back porch, as was my custom, and headed towards the mirador. As on other days, I was obliged to pass the area where the building work was underway. The workmen had already emptied the rooms on the ground floor and were in the process of dismantling the partition walls. They were using heavy iron hammers, and the rhythm of their blows and the noise of the rubble caused me to stop by one of the doors to watch what they were doing. The walls can't have been very resistant because they gave way easily to the battering they received. It was then, as I watched with the interest of someone seeing such work for the first time, that one of the men stopped hitting the wall and shouted:

'Hang on a minute! What have we here?'

The other workmen put down their tools and went over to where he was standing. I also entered the building, drawn by curiosity. The man had started demolishing an inner wall which appeared to separate two rooms and had just discovered this wasn't so: each room had its own partition and between them both was a small compartment, a strange cubby-hole a couple of feet wide. Even I realized this wasn't normal. The one who seemed to be the foreman went up to the partially demolished walls and peered into the space between them. There can't have been enough light because he went to fetch a torch and, turning it on, he proceeded to examine the chamber.

'There's something in there,' he said. 'Carry on knocking down the walls, but do it carefully, working from the inside.'

With smaller hammers, two men continued dismantling the brick walls. And I stayed watching them, suddenly intrigued to find out what could be inside that compartment which appeared to have no set function.

Once both the walls had been brought down to a height of barely two feet, the workmen stopped. Everyone leaned forwards to see what was inside the gap, and so did I. The light coming in through the windows now reached to the back of that small space.

The skull was the first thing I noticed. I'd never seen one before and couldn't help feeling disgusted. It emerged from the top of a rolled-up carpet which filled the cavity, and it seemed to observe us with irritation and surprise through both its sockets, as if it were none too pleased to be suddenly exposed to the light of day.

'There's a dead body!' exclaimed one of the builders.

'And look! There's a hole in its skull,' added another standing next to me.

This comment drew my attention to something I hadn't noticed. In the skull's left temple was a circular opening, a hole which, probably from watching so many films, I recognized immediately. You didn't have to be very intelligent to realize this hole was the result of a bullet entering the skull. I remember the amazement I felt, an amazement shared by the workmen who'd just unearthed these remains.

'Don't touch anything!' ordered the foreman. 'We have to leave everything as it is and inform Don Víctor as quickly as possible.'

'My father's in Coruña and won't be back until one thirty,' I explained. Although we were on holiday, Daddy carried on going to his notary's office in July, but was always back in time for lunch.

'Then we have to let Dona Flora know. She can ring him, we'd better not let anyone else know until Don Víctor has been informed.'

The foreman sent one of the workers off to fetch my mother. The man came back quite soon, but my mother took longer. Although she must have been prepared for what she was about to see, she couldn't avoid a look of amazement, as had happened to the rest of us a moment before. But she soon recovered and adopted the role assigned to her, no doubt she felt she ought to take control of the situation in front of the workmen.

'I have just spoken to my husband on the phone and he gave me instructions as to what must be done in such cases.' It amused me to see the air of determination she gave herself, so different from the way she was normally at home, when my father was about. 'I've telephoned the Civil Guard, who are responsible for informing the judge. We're not to touch anything until the judge arrives.'

Shortly after that, the Civil Guard pulled up in a car. Three officers got out and, having verified the discovery was real, told us the judge would be here soon. While we waited, one of them started taking photographs of the compartment and adjoining rooms. I was so absorbed by what was going on I didn't even notice the hours go by; in my memory the events followed each other quickly, though there must have been a significant amount of time spent waiting in between.

My father arrived before the judge, having possibly left Coruña as soon as he heard from Mummy. In his presence the builders and officers adopted an attitude of submission, as if they were at his orders. I'd witnessed such behaviour before, but was always amazed by the respect with which my father was treated in town, as if subjection to the lord of the manor had been inscribed in the DNA of the people of Vilarelle since time immemorial.

He also checked the discovery was real and confirmed we had to wait for the judge, only he could order the removal of the body or what was left of it. The judge soon arrived. He was a young man, tall, with a pronounced bald spot which didn't give him the distinguished air I'd been expecting. He was quite different from the typical image I had of a judge, elderly and serious-looking, and was accompanied by a man I later learned was the legal secretary and a woman younger than my mother, who turned out to be the coroner.

Although they must all have been completely used to the procedures followed in such cases, I felt like the spectator of a film being projected before my eyes. In a serious tone, as if addressing someone who wasn't there, the judge described out loud what the rest of us could see. The secretary stood next to him and noted down everything he said. I was struck by the judge's description, the cold, precise language which, at a distance, conveyed the terrible reality we were facing. Once this was over, he ordered the rolled-up carpet to be removed so that he could examine what was inside, something it wasn't difficult to guess.

The builders dismantled the rest of the walls as carefully as if they were carving a delicate sculpture. Once the walls were down, the officers proceeded to extract the carpet and placed it in an area we quickly vacated. The carpet disintegrated slightly when it was removed, it must have been all mouldy after so long in that compartment. When they rolled it out, they found what I think we'd all imagined: a whole skeleton in a good state of preservation.

You could still see the remnants of the clothes the person had been wearing when they were shut up in that strange chamber, but many years must have passed because only the bones were well preserved, despite some of them being loose. As the judge continued his meticulous description of the scene, I was able to observe certain details I would have missed otherwise: the buckle and remains of what must once have been a leather belt, several buttons from the trousers and shirt worn by the deceased, as well as the rubber soles of the shoes, the only materials which had withstood the devastating effect of time.

Then the coroner knelt down and rummaged among the bones. Using some pincers, she picked out the buttons and remains of the belt, which the officers sealed in some clear plastic bags. She also located a thin chain, which hadn't been visible at first, together with a blackened medallion. Finally, having examined the skull, she pulled out a small piece of metal. As she was now describing what she found, I learned this was the bullet which had made a hole in the skull. She then poked in among the ribs and pulled out another piece of metal similar to the first. Two bullets, clear evidence that the person to whom this skeleton belonged had died as a result of two gunshot wounds, a death which could hardly be considered natural.

Having conferred in a low voice with the coroner, the judge described the skeleton as that of a young man a little under six feet tall, who had probably been buried there for more than fifty years. He described the hole in the skull and the crack in one of the back ribs, which must have suffered the impact of the second bullet. Finally he gave an overview of the place and circumstances in which the remains had come to light.

Once the authorities had finished their work, the officer took a few more photographs of the skeleton and the place where it had been found. Then two men entered the building, who until that point had been waiting outside. They placed the carpet and remains on a stretcher, which they introduced into a vehicle parked nearby. From the workmen's conversations, I learned they were from the undertaker's in Vilarelle and would take the remains to the town's mortuary. My father, who meanwhile had been talking to the judge and coroner, went with them since he'd been asked to go to the courthouse and fill out a few forms. My mother went back into the house to see to the lunch and, since it was now after two, the builders collected their things and left for the day, my father having told them there was no need for them to work that afternoon.

I was left alone, still confused by all the events I'd just witnessed. I felt strange, not only as a result of seeing a skeleton for the first time, but because, while I couldn't put it into words exactly, it was obvious something unusual had happened. Someone had shot a man twice and then concealed the corpse behind a wall. It sounded like a story from one of the mystery books I'd been reading, a story which might take place in a damp and misty London, for example, but never in our family home.

I approached the small compartment again, this peculiar tomb which had held a corpse for so many years. At the back of it, there was only dust and a few scraps from the carpet. The builders would soon dismantle everything and rearrange that space as if there'd never been a body. There's nothing easier than erasing all traces of the things we would rather forget.

As I turned to leave, my eyes fell on a small object in the area where they'd rolled out the carpet, half hidden by the rubble. I knelt down to pick it up and placed it in the palm of my hand: it was a ring, a simple ring made of a dark grey metal. It grew wider at the top, where it formed an oval, inside which an ornate letter 'R' had been engraved.

Without quite knowing why, I took the decision to keep it for myself, though it would have been more reasonable to hand it over to my parents, since it wasn't difficult to surmise that this object had belonged to the person whose remains had just been brought to light. I didn't think at the time that I might be concealing evidence or something like that, nor was I aware of the importance the ring would have. I simply acted on impulse and, going on my diary entry for that day, out of a predisposition to fantasy and a certain desire that this unexpected discovery would help me to escape the routine awaiting me that summer.

3

When I entered the dining room, everyone was already sitting at the table. The twins and Alfredo didn't stop complaining about missing the discovery of the skeleton, which they'd heard all about, and all through lunch they kept cracking sinister jokes. My cousin Ana, on the other hand, adopted an expression of disgust and horror, the same as my mother, who refused to eat because she said she'd lost her appetite after what she'd seen. My father was the only one who ate well and, the few times he joined in the conversation, it was to rebuke my brothers or play down the importance of what he always referred to as 'that unfortunate incident'.

After lunch I withdrew to my room, pretending I wanted to rest a little. I did this every day because around that time I liked to be alone in my bedroom and listen to my own music, in particular the Clash's incendiary songs, which went so well with the vague sense of unease I'd been feeling for months. As it was hot, I left the window open and half-closed the shutters. My room was on the first floor of the side wing and looked out onto the back of the house; from it I could go through a glass door and reach a terrace which stretched all along the main wing of the building. Under the terrace was an area surrounded by pillars, an ideal place to seek shade when the weather was hot. Next to it, two bougainvilleas climbed up the wall, creating a green and violet ceiling which made that spot the most pleasant of all. That was where my parents must have been drinking coffee because I could hear their voices as clearly as if they were in my bedroom. Under any other circumstances I wouldn't have paid attention, but I pricked up my ears when I realized they were talking about the skeleton which had been unearthed that morning.

'There's no need to wait for the coroner's report to guess what happened,' my mother was saying. 'You've the two bullets and the hole in the skull. It was clearly a murder, Víctor.'

'So what if it was?' my father answered in a sharp tone he rarely used at home, especially with my mother.

'Well, somebody killed him and then walled him up. You have to think it was someone from the manor house.'

'What does that mean? Why does it have to be someone from the manor house?' My father could barely contain his anger.

'If not from the manor house, someone who knew it well,' my mother corrected herself. 'It's not as if the corpse was buried in the garden or wood. You can't just build a wall in five seconds; whoever did it must have had access to the store, the materials.'

'Who cares how it happened? Listen, Flora, you heard what the judge said. That body had been there for more than fifty years. I wasn't even born back then!'

'But your parents were. And your grandparents, obviously. Didn't they live here around that time? I don't mean they had anything to do with it, don't get me wrong, but they may have known something about what happened.'

'What nonsense! How can you even think that?' My father grew more irritated. Then, after a brief silence, he added, 'If it was during the Civil War, as seems to be the case from the dates, it could have been anyone. I understand that in August 1936 my grandparents went to live in Santiago and didn't return until the following summer, when things here had calmed down. That was when my father joined the army, so I don't expect he spent much time in the manor.'

'What about the servants? There must have been people looking after the house and grounds.'

'Stop fantasizing, Flora, it's not worth it. I spoke to the judge on the way to the courthouse. Do you know who his father is? Alberto Riquer, a notary in Ferrol, a colleague who owes me more than one favour,' my father's voice had regained the pleasant tone with which he usually addressed Mummy. 'He already told me not to worry; if the deceased had been there for so many years, the case had prescribed and the proceedings would be filed away somewhere. So who cares about a few bones? To me they're like an archaeological find of the sort you get when digging foundations. I sympathize with the deceased, whoever he was, but it has nothing to do with us. The best thing we can do is forget about that unfortunate incident.'

My parents carried on discussing the events for some time, but all they did was repeat their arguments using other words. In the end they agreed to try to avoid news of the events spreading: the last thing they wanted was some journalist finding out and sullying the good name of the

Soutelos. Daddy was going to ask the judge to be discreet and see if he couldn't have a word with the coroner, other employees and Civil Guard officers. He'd also make sure the workmen didn't wag their tongues about it. He would obviously use all his influence to stop news getting out and to handle the affair as carefully as possible. Knowing him as I did, I was convinced he'd bury the skeleton under so much earth, this time it'd never be found.

After they left and it became silent, I lay on the bed, going over what I'd just heard. I couldn't stop thinking about some of the things my mother had said. The body clearly pointed to a murder. This means there must have been a murderer and it was logical to suspect someone who'd lived in the manor house or had access to it. A murderer in my family tree? I was young then, with plenty of time on my hands, I suppose it was normal my imagination should run away with me. But if my father had anything to do with it, the mystery would never be investigated.

I put my hand in my pocket and felt the ring I'd found that morning, which I'd almost forgotten about. I took it out and gazed at it with curiosity, aware that this small object could be a thread with which to pull on the skein which, without my realizing, was already forming in my head. Who did the corpse belong to? The coroner's analyses might help to clear it up and then it would come to light, even though the information was kept in the small circle my father decided.

But there had to be a murderer as well, and I couldn't tell if this was someone from inside my family or outside it.

A stranger to me in either case. Of the previous inhabitants of the manor, I'd only ever known my grandmother Rosalía, since my grandfather had died soon after I was born and I only recognized him from the photos in some of the rooms. I knew nothing about my more distant relatives, starting with my great-grandparents who Daddy had spoken about. To me they were just figures I saw in a few group portraits which had been framed and hung on the wall. Sometimes, over lunch, I'd heard names and references, but I'd never been that interested; with the exception of my grandparents and my uncle and aunt, I was completely ignorant about all my father's family.

Intrigued, I stood up and walked to the library, which was also on the first floor. I went in and found the place in shadow, since the shutters to the terrace and windows overlooking the front were closed. A few rays of light filtered through the cracks in the wood, intruders who'd come to play with the specks of dust which seemed to float inside them. The atmosphere was stifling, it was obvious no one had bothered to air the room for days. I opened the doors to the terrace so the light and air could enter freely. Then I searched on the shelf where I knew the family photo albums were kept. Instead of examining those with photos from my father's childhood, I focused my attention on three volumes of older photos, most of them a faded brown colour which clearly indicated the intervening years.

Although there were a few individual ones, they were mostly group portraits. I couldn't help shivering when I considered how one of these faces peering at me from the depths of time could hide the look of an assassin.

How to know if I had no clues to go on? Just the ring, if that really was a clue. All the same, if I wanted to know more, I'd have to take the initiative. This mystery could help to brighten up the summer which lay ahead of me.

I took the ring out of my pocket again. Looking at it closely, I decided it could well be made of silver; next to my bed, I had a medallion I'd been given as a young girl, which had acquired the same dark grey colour. I remembered seeing Luz, the maid we had in Coruña, cleaning the silver in the sitting room with a special liquid. There had to be something similar in the manor house which would allow me to restore the ring to its former glory.

I left the library and went down to the kitchen. Celsa the cook was still putting away the crockery from lunch. She was always pleased to see me, I'd been her favourite since I was a child; she loved taking care of me. She was surprised by my request, but didn't say anything. She opened a drawer in the cupboard and took out a small bottle and cloth. She told me what I had to do and asked me to return the things when I'd finished with them.

Back in my bedroom, I poured a few drops of the cleaning liquid onto the cloth and used it to rub the ring. After I'd gone over the surface several times, the silver started to shine again like new. The letter 'R' could now be clearly seen inside the oval, the only decoration on the ring, which was otherwise simply made. This letter could be the initial of a name, some of my friends had rings just like it. The first which came to my mind was Rosalía, my grandmother's name, but I quickly realized this was a pretty hazardous guess. There were lots of names beginning with

'R' and no reason why a ring belonging to my grandmother should turn up next to that corpse.

I was drawn to the mystery opening before me, but also frustrated, since I had no idea how to solve it. Now that I'm older, I have a more elaborate version of events; as I describe them now, without wanting to, I may be introducing details I didn't find out until later. Because when I reread what I wrote in my diary that evening, all I find is a bewildered and superficial account of the corpse's discovery. But I must have sensed something even then, since I also wrote the following:

Of course, apart from what we discovered (a corpse with two bullets inside it, does a skeleton count as a corpse?), there's also what we didn't discover, since there's no murder without a murderer. Could it have something to do with our family, some ancestor of mine? Given that the dead don't speak, we may never know. How I wish Sherlock Holmes were here, I'd happily play the role of Dr Watson, to see if he had as much success as in his novels.

4

If I can trust the notes in my diary, it was three days after the discovery of the skeleton that I had my first meeting with Miguel. The truth is I don't need to refer to what I wrote that day in order clearly to remember the afternoon I spoke to him for the first time; there are moments in life which are never erased and remain firmly anchored in our memories.

I've already said how much I liked to while away the hours in the mirador at the other end of the wood. The mirador could also be reached by following a track through the orchard to a path which ran alongside the river, very near the enclosure wall. Sitting on the stone bench, the trees forming a thick barrier behind me and the honeysuckle protecting me from unwanted glances, I had the impression I was on a desert island.

From the mirador, since there weren't many fruit trees on that side, I could see the meadows sloping down to the river. There wasn't a river as such on Soutelo land, just part of one: a stream which rose to the surface far away, in one of the mountains on the horizon, and was already swollen when it entered our property through an arch in the wall and continued for several hundred yards before leaving through another arch and heading for the town, which it curved around. Along one of its banks grew willows and alders which, together with the wall behind, marked the lower boundary of the estate.

That afternoon I'd been immersed in *Great Expectations*, the novel by Charles Dickens with which I'd decided to start my summer reading, when in an area close to the wall, where there were some plum trees, I saw a boy up in one of the trees. Lodged between two branches, he was busy picking the ripest plums, which he dropped into a plastic bag. Intrigued, I left the book on the bench and crept over to where he was, trying to make as little noise as possible. He can't have heard me approach, he was so busy, because he almost fell out of the tree when I started speaking.

'May I know what you're doing up there? Were you never taught to respect what isn't yours?'

The boy twisted around and observed me. He was so surprised he seemed to blush, but he quickly recovered. He slid down the tree, left the bag on the ground and turned to face me. He must have been a good few inches taller than I was. What caught my attention most, if my memory doesn't fail me, were his eyes, a blue-grey colour, and his ruffled hair, which he tried to arrange using his fingers as a makeshift comb.

'You've plenty of fruit, you always let it rot,' he answered in what struck me as an aggressive tone. 'I come and pick it every summer, it's a shame to let it go to waste. When there are chestnuts, I visit the grove as well.'

'And how do you get in? Didn't you know this is private property?'

'Yes, but until you fix that wall, I'll carry on coming in through there,' he pointed to a section of the wall where the top had partly disintegrated, which it must have been pretty easy to climb over from outside. Then, as if he felt obliged to justify his behaviour, he insisted, 'There's plenty of fruit, none of you picks it. It's a shame to let it rot.'

'None of us?' I answered, still amazed by the natural way the boy was confronting the situation. 'Who do you mean?'

'Those in the manor house, who else? I know it's been bought by Don Víctor and there are people living in it.'

'Don Víctor? How do you know him?'

'In Vilarelle everyone knows who's in the manor house, though the person I knew best was Dona Rosalía. She saw me in the garden lots of times when I was younger and never said a word.'

Then he looked me up and down and asked:

'So who are you?'

'Don't you think I should be asking you that question?' I replied, taken aback by the way the conversation was going.

'My name is Miguel, though I don't suppose you're that interested. I live in one of the houses just outside the town. You can see it from the wall, it can't be half a mile from here.'

'Well, my name is Clara,' I said after an awkward silence. 'Dona Rosalía, as you call her, was my grandmother. And that Don Víctor you talk about is my father. So now you know.'

'In theory that means we're almost neighbours. Though in practice it's as if we lived thousands of miles apart,' there was irony in his voice and in the smile flickering across his lips.

'Why do you say that?'

'Mine is a humble abode, miss,' he said the word 'miss' with a sarcasm which hurt and made me feel suddenly irritated by this boy who looked at me as if stealing fruit from the manor were the most natural thing in the world. 'The distance between poor and rich can be huge, I suppose you'll have learned that at that expensive school you probably go to.'

There he was, proud and defiant, with a smug look on his face. He should have been apologizing for being caught stealing fruit, and yet I was the one who seemed to need to justify myself.

'What is it? Must I apologize for being born into my family? Well, if you're so smart, you should know that's not something you choose,' I answered roughly. 'Now please leave. I think you have enough fruit for today.'

'Whatever you say, Miss Scarlet,' he replied mockingly, imitating the voice of the black slave in *Gone with the Wind*. He walked over to the wall, lifted the bag over, scampered up the stones and disappeared from view.

This meeting put me in a bad mood for the rest of the day. I must still have been annoyed in the evening, judging by what I wrote in my diary. I read the entry now and it seems strange, unfair even, perhaps because I'm influenced by what happened next or because I was already unwilling to admit how drawn I was to Miguel's appearance and self-confidence:

I had a very strange meeting this afternoon. A boy from the town, who was older than me, came to steal from the estate. I found him picking plums as if they belonged to him. I remarked on this and, instead of taking to his heels, he began to answer me back as if I were the one who should be apologizing. He behaved in an arrogant and very unpleasant way, making me feel guilty for my remarks and for living in the manor. If all the boys of Vilarelle are as horrible as him, I prefer to stay shut up here all summer. Brave fool! I hope our paths never cross again.

Despite what I wrote, this first meeting must have left me feeling something other than anger because two days later I was strangely elated when I saw him again. It was a Saturday morning and the sun was shining. Nobody in my family was up, but I'd woken early and, after a breakfast of toast and coffee served to me by Celsa in the kitchen, I decided to go for a bike ride in the wood.

I've already said that the manor grounds were extensive. Behind the allotments, on the western side of the building, began the wood which, were it not for the enclosure wall, would have seemed as immense to me as the forests in fairy tales. It was there I decided to roam that morning, in search of an unexplored corner.

I pedalled for some time along the narrow alleys between chestnut trees and oaks. The rays of sunlight still hadn't penetrated the foliage and the air was as fresh as at night. Although I was wearing a thin jersey, I soon felt frozen, so I decided to leave the wood and follow the track through the meadows down to the river. There was a spot I particularly liked, where the river opened out and formed a kind of natural swimming pool, protected from the sun by the alders on the other side. I was only a few yards from my destination when I noticed the presence of Miguel standing motionless next to the river, with a fishing rod in his hand. He heard me coming this time, but all he did was turn his head and nod by way of greeting.

'Hello, Clara,' he said when I reached him. 'It was Clara, wasn't it? It's still early. I thought you rich folk stayed in bed. Have you come to tell me off again?'

'Well, look who's here!' I exclaimed. There was not a trace of irony in his voice, but in mine there was, as if I wished to take revenge for the humiliation I'd felt the other day. 'The fruit thief! And now the trout thief. I suppose you know this part of the river belongs to the manor.'

'My name is Miguel, as I told you before. And in case you hadn't realized, the river belongs to everyone. The fact that this stretch of the river is inside the estate is an injustice which will be corrected one day.' He changed his tone of voice, which had become defiant, and added calmly, 'Besides, this is one of the best places to fish for trout.'

'To steal them, you mean,' I insisted.

'I'm not stealing here. You're not going to be ruined by a few trout which a few minutes ago were swimming outside these grounds. Besides, who's to say you aren't the thieves? You or the law which allows part of the river to be on private property.'

I chose not to reply to his impertinent remarks, perhaps because deep down there was a lot of truth in what he was saying. I noticed to my surprise that my anger of the other day had vanished. I may have found it difficult to admit, but I wanted to talk to this boy who was so sure of himself and seemed to have an answer for everything.

'I'm not going to report you, don't worry.' I leaned the bike against a bench next to the track and turned to Miguel with a conciliatory air, 'Are they biting then?'

'They would if you'd keep quiet and not stand so close. Trout are clever, they won't come if they sense our presence. But I've caught five today, aren't they amazing?'

He showed me the sack he'd placed on the grass, in the bottom of which he'd prepared a bed of fern. There were five beautiful trout, with shiny, slippery skin and those dark orange spots all along their backs, though I was sorry they were no longer alive.

'As soon as I catch another, I'll stop. Six are enough to feed three persons. See, just as in the old days, when a man had to return home with just the right amount of food.'

I fell silent and stood still, as he'd asked, watching the bobbing of the float on the water's surface. It wasn't long before another trout bit. I was surprised by the way the float suddenly dipped, the line grew tense and Miguel quickly reacted. The trout jumped into the air, desperately wagging its tail. But all its attempts were useless. Miguel moved the rod, lowered the fish onto the grass and held it with one hand, while removing the hook with the other. He dropped it into the sack, where it carried on flapping, though all the time it was losing strength. Then, as he'd promised, Miguel collected his things, folded the fishing rod and went to sit on the bench where I'd left my bike.

'So you're Don Víctor's daughter,' he said, inviting me to sit next to him. 'Why haven't I seen you in the manor before?'

'We didn't use to visit very often, only to see my grandmother. And when she died, we stopped coming. Until this summer, that is.'

Miguel fell silent and gazed at me with an intensity which made me look away.

'When you were small, did you have long hair?'

'Yes, I did. I had it cut three years ago,' I replied.

'Now I recognize you! You were very pretty as a girl. I remember often looking at you, it was impossible not to notice you. But you always appeared very distant.'

'So I was very pretty as a girl,' I answered ironically. 'Well, thanks for the compliment, even if it's a little overdue.'

Miguel stared at me for a few moments which seemed to go on for ever. I ended up looking away again, disturbed by the effect his gaze had on me.

'The truth is you've changed a lot,' he added with a smile. 'And I'd say it was for the better.'

'I'm not the only one who's changed,' I replied, trying to hide the sensation of pleasure his words had given me. 'The other day you addressed me as your enemy, but I see you know how to be pleasant as well.'

'Don't worry, the other day was nothing personal. It may even be true you're not to blame for coming from the manor.'

'You're always on about the same, I don't know what you have against my family,' I protested, deeply satisfied that he'd remembered my remarks.

'What I have against your family? How can you ask that? You're rich and can do whatever you like. You don't know what it is to wish for something and not have it. You behave as if the world was yours and the rest of us didn't exist.'

I was about to answer his angry discourse, but he left me with the words in my mouth. He explained it was late and he still had lots to do. He picked up the trout and fishing rod and headed towards the section of the wall he'd climbed over the first time we'd met. After about twenty yards, he turned around and said:

'Goodbye, Clara. We'll be seeing each other, I plan to come and steal again.'

I sat on the bench and watched him leave without saying anything. I cursed my inability to prolong a conversation which had been much shorter than I would have liked. I felt happy inside, a strange happiness which surprised me. At least this time he hadn't called me Miss Scarlet and his words had seemed less aggressive than before. I wanted to talk more to this Miguel who was so different from all the boys I knew at school, but I'd have to wait for another opportunity. The summer would be long and he'd promised to return.

5

I saw Miguel the next day, twice in fact. The first time was in the morning, unexpectedly. Over breakfast my mother reminded me I owed her a favour I couldn't refuse. Soon after we'd arrived, she'd promised to go and pay Adelaida Novo a visit in her home and, since the latter hadn't stopped insisting, she'd decided to fulfil her obligation that morning. The Novo family was very influential in town; they lived in Madrid during the year, but every summer without fail they returned to their house in Vilarelle. Mummy wanted me to go with her; I suppose my presence there would serve as an excuse to avoid a possible invitation to lunch or some other awkward situation.

On the way she planned to take her Volkswagen Golf to the garage. It had needed to be serviced for several weeks. In Coruña she hadn't had time, she explained, and everything was that much easier in Vilarelle. I suppose what she meant is that, being the lady of the manor, she was sure she'd be seen to immediately, even if there were twenty other customers waiting in line.

We dropped the car off first of all. While Mummy was talking to the manager, who quickly mobilized half of humanity to look after her, I moved away and amused myself seeing what was there. It was then I spotted Miguel. He was at the back of the garage, leaning against a red

Citroën which had the bonnet up. He was wearing blue overalls, like the other employees, and holding a torch over the engine, which another mechanic seemed to be trying to fix. I stopped a few feet away, taking in the scene, unsure what to do.

It wasn't long before he sensed my presence. I quickly noticed it made him feel uncomfortable, even angry that I should see him like this, in oil-stained overalls with a torch in his hand. I nodded and smiled while walking towards him, but Miguel returned my greeting with a severe expression and focused his attention on the engine, as if it were the most important thing in the world and my presence there deserved only a brief interruption.

After leaving the garage, Mummy and I headed for the Novos' house. It couldn't be compared to the manor, needless to say, the difference was immense, but it was one of the town's most beautiful buildings, a mansion built in the colonial style which is still easy to find in lots of places in Galicia. It was near the park, in the middle of a small garden, and stood out at a distance because of the elegant tower which rose on the right of the building.

I regretted accompanying my mother as soon as we arrived. Not because of Dona Adelaida, who was waiting for us and made every effort to see to our needs, or rather to see to the two housemaids who rushed in and out carrying trays laden with snacks. The one who put me in a bad mood was her daughter, Teté. She was my age and I realized, when we started talking, she was just as unbearable as she had been when a child.

While our mothers chatted in the drawing room, I was forced to accompany her to her room, which was decorated in different shades of pink and covered with posters of the kind of smoochy singers I despised. No doubt she'd have died of fright if she'd been able to see the huge poster in my bedroom, the impressive cover of *London Calling* by the Clash, with Paul Simonon smashing his bass against the stage and Joe Strummer watching from a few steps behind. A poster I've kept, despite its poor condition, since I haven't stopped listening to the Clash all these years.

It soon became clear Teté saw in me not a girl of her own age, but a representative of the Soutelo family tree. She fell over backwards trying to please me, as if I were somehow superior. I felt like explaining to her we were just two girls forced to put up with each other, but I remembered my mother's warning before we left and decided to cope as best I could. The worst thing was she insisted so much I had to invite her to spend an afternoon in the manor. In return she promised to call me to join the group of boys and girls formed by those who spent the summer in Vilarelle and the children of some of the more well-to-do families who lived there all year round. A prospect I didn't relish, which I tried to keep vague, in the hope it would never happen.

Once she felt we were getting on well, Teté adopted a conspiratorial look and said to me:

'I know all about the corpse you found at home. I'm told you were there when it was discovered. What was it like? Is it true there were several bullet holes in its skull?'

Well, blow me down, I thought when she asked me. That was all I needed, having to give explanations about something I considered my personal secret. I answered all her questions with monosyllables, without offering her any more information than I judged she already knew. She drove me crazy with her insistence on the number of bullets (six according to her; obviously the exaggerations had begun) and who could have committed the crime. I was especially annoyed that she should use the word 'crime', but the truth is she was right, I thought the same. Crime or murder, what difference did it make? She asked me so many questions I got to the conclusion she'd prepared the interrogation with her mother beforehand, I was sure they were capable of this. I dodged as many as I could and tried to play the whole thing down, though the questions she asked were exactly the same I'd been obsessed with since the day the skeleton was discovered.

My mother came to rescue me when I was on the verge of a nervous attack. I left the house with relief, as if I'd struggled free from a sticky and unpleasant cobweb. Luckily Mummy made no reference to the skeleton, it may not have come up in her conversation, or it had and she preferred to forget about it. In any case she seemed to feel the same relief I felt on leaving the Novos' house. Mummy didn't mind having a social life, especially when she had to go somewhere with Daddy, but she preferred being at home, with her paintings. She could have been different, it would have been reasonable to expect her to make the most of the privileged social position she enjoyed as lady of the manor, especially in town. But for once luck was on my side.

After our brief meeting in the garage, I thought I wouldn't see Miguel again for quite some time. But I was wrong, we met again that same afternoon. I was sitting in the mirador, as on other occasions, reading the novel I'd begun when we arrived at the manor house. I looked up on hearing a noise and it was then I noticed Miguel's head and arms appearing over the wall, in the exact place he'd come in other times. When he realized he'd been spotted, he fell back down on the other side. The last thing I wanted was for him to leave, so I raised my voice and asked:

'What? You thieves not working today?'

After a little, I saw his hands and then his head reappear over the wall. He finished climbing and with an athletic leap landed in our property. I put my book down and gestured to him to come over.

'The apples around here are still green, but there's some ripe fruit on the pear trees,' I said as soon as he was close. I adopted a tone which was both sarcastic and friendly; I suppose it must have been obvious I was pleased to see him. 'Don't hold back for my sake, pretend I'm invisible.'

'You can see I don't even have a bag with me, I haven't come to pick anything today,' he replied neutrally. 'Or I have, depends how you look at it.'

'What do you mean?'

'Well, I wanted to come and see if you were here. But don't worry; if I'm bothering you, I'll leave straightaway.'

'Stay if you like. Then at least we can talk a little. The other day you took off like a ghost!' For the first time, I smiled at him openly. 'I wouldn't want to waste a thief's day off.'

Miguel came over to the bench and sat next to me. He took the book I'd put down and examined it carefully:

'*Great Expectations* by old Dickens. That's a good book, yes siree. I liked it a lot when I read it.'

'You've read this book?' I asked, unable to conceal my amazement.

'I have. Workers read as well, you know,' he'd abandoned his pleasant expression and regained the defiant tone of our first meetings. 'Strange beasts, like others out there and about. I think *National Geographic* is preparing a documentary on us.'

'That's not what I meant, don't be so hasty,' I lied. In fact Miguel had guessed my thoughts immediately.

'It doesn't matter, don't worry. To tell the truth, you're right,' his voice was back to normal. 'Among my friends, I'm the only one who couldn't live without reading.'

'It's the same with the rich, you know. Or do you think I have lots of friends who read Dickens?'

He didn't answer. He just gazed at me and smiled. His look gave me the same sensation of pleasure as the other day, I don't know what it was made those blue eyes of his so special. To hide my feelings, I added:

'How come you started reading? You know what they say: it's a vice someone has to give you. I picked it up from an uncle of mine called Carlos, and from my mother. She loves books; when I was small, she used to read me stories in bed. She likes to say she was my Scheherazade. We still talk a lot about books we've read.'

'Well, now we're making our confessions, it's something I received in inheritance from my great-grandfather, a man

I only ever met in photos, strange way to pick something up. His name was Ishmael and he was a bookbinder. Quite a character, and I say that not just because he was my great-grandfather.'

'"Call me Ishmael,"' I said almost automatically, adopting a theatrical air.

'Don't think you're so clever! I've also read *Moby Dick*.' He grinned at my exclamation of surprise; I was amazed he'd recognized the opening line of Melville's novel. After a brief silence, he went on, 'You know I was almost called Ishmael as well? That was what my mother and grandmother wanted. But my father was dead set against it, and I ended up being Miguel. Not so literary, but not bad either.'

I remained quiet, I didn't know what to say. I was taken aback by this boy who was so different from others I'd met. There was nothing predictable about him, I never knew where he was going. His next question also took me by surprise:

'Is it true you discovered a skeleton in the manor house? Talking of my grandmother reminded me of it.'

'We did, yes, on the ground floor where the store used to be. How did you find out about it?'

'I don't think there's a single house in Vilarelle where it hasn't been talked about. You may not have realized yet, but what goes on in the manor is always important in town.' As I didn't venture to speak, busy as I was observing every detail of his eyes, he continued, 'It was in the newspaper as well, just a single column, all hidden away. We wouldn't want to publicize events at the manor if they're not pleasant, if they're going to sully the Soutelos' good name.'

When he adopted this attitude, Miguel was contemptible. There seemed to be a vein of hatred inside him which came out at the first opportunity. A vein of hatred which made me uncomfortable because it acted like a barrier which prevented me from reaching him. Now, when I think about it after all these years, I have the impression he felt uncomfortable as well because I didn't fit the mould of someone belonging to a family such as mine. As I didn't want our conversation to continue along these lines, I decided to change subject:

'You said before your great-grandfather Ishmael was quite a character. What made him so special?'

My question caught him by surprise and I saw he hesitated before answering. I moved a little closer to him in an unconscious attempt to provoke a reply. After a silence which seemed to me eternal, he replied:

'I only know what my grandmother told me. I never met him, he died in 1954, years before I was born. He worked as a bookbinder, books were his passion. He was never able to study, Vilarelle only had a primary school. But he read everything which fell into his hands: novels, poetry, history... You have to see the books he kept in his trunk, they're the only ones which were saved.'

'Saved? What do you mean?'

'My great-grandfather was a Republican. He ran a cultural association for workers before the Civil War. He discussed his ideas freely, he thought what this country needed was bread and books. Which is why, when Civil War broke out in 1936, he was one of the first the soldiers arrested.'

I remained quiet and lowered my head, like a child who's been caught at school without their homework. For a moment I thought Miguel would leave, as on the day he came fishing, but after a while he carried on with his story:

'When they came to arrest him, the Falangists took all the books they found in the house and in his workshop and made a bonfire with them in the middle of the street. They missed the books in his trunk in the attic. My great-grandfather had foreseen what would happen and hidden his favourite books there.'

I was deeply impressed by what I'd heard. It's not that I was ignorant about the Spanish Civil War, I'd read several novels set during that period. I hadn't learned much at school since, every time we studied history or literature, the world seemed to come to an end just before 1936 and we never studied the final chapters in the books. But this was the first time someone had spoken to me about the war from family memories – in the flesh, as it were. What Miguel had told me had happened to his great-grandfather, had happened in Vilarelle, the last place I imagined them burning books, something I'd seen in films set in Nazi Germany.

'You said they arrested your great-grandfather. What for?'

'I bet they don't teach you that at the rich school you go to,' the aggressive tone of irony I already knew resurfaced in Miguel's voice, but it only lasted a moment before he added, 'Excuse me, I shouldn't have said that. They don't teach it at rich schools or any others. I never had it explained to me, anyway. If I know something about that period, it's what I was told at home. He was arrested for being a Republican, for running a cultural association, for reading too many books... any old reason, I suppose. But I don't like talking about it, I start to feel really angry. And the one who knows the story well is my grandmother, you'd like her, I'm sure.'

We must have been sitting for ages, though the hours had gone by without my noticing. The sun was low in the sky and the air was fresher. The two of us remained quiet, perhaps thinking the conversation had come to an end. But after a while Miguel decided to take it up again:

'It's the way things are. You know these last few days my grandmother hasn't stopped talking about the Republic. Mum says it's because of that corpse you discovered, she probably associates it with back then. Lots of people died when the war started, that must be why.'

'Well, I'd like to meet her, I'm sure the stories she tells are very interesting,' I remarked in order to say something.

'They are. You know she also talks a lot about your grandmother Rosalía. Says she was the prettiest girl around.'

'And do you think your grandmother would want to speak to me?' I ventured to ask. After the reference to Grandma Rosalía, I began to notice a sudden interest even I didn't quite understand.

'If there's something my grandmother likes, it's talking. I'm sure she'd love to tell you all her stories. Of course that would mean coming to my house. It's up to you. Do you think you could stand seeing how the other half lives?'

There he was again, being satirical. But I decided not to pay any attention and to focus on what it was I wanted. We soon agreed on the details of my future visit. When Miguel left and disappeared behind the wall, I stayed in the mirador for a while, going over the long conversation we'd had. I felt strangely euphoric and for the first time I was glad circumstances obliged me to spend that summer shut up in the family home.

6

The next day, after lunch, I went to meet Miguel as we'd agreed the previous evening. To avoid awkward questions, since people would notice if I left through the front door, I pretended to follow my usual routine. I took my copy of *Great Expectations* and said I was going for a walk in the wood. I was afraid someone might be surprised to see me in trainers and jeans, instead of the shorts I wore most days, but nobody gave it another thought.

Miguel was waiting for me inside the estate, sitting on the grass, with his back against the enclosure wall. He must have been there for quite some time, since lunch had been delayed and I was running late. For the first time in our acquaintance, he greeted me normally; I was almost surprised there was no hint of irony in his words, and grateful not to have to be on the alert all the time. He helped me to climb over the wall where it had partly collapsed and then jumped over himself. As soon as I was outside the manor grounds, I felt the excitement which always came over me when doing something which was not allowed; because, as far as my family was concerned, this meeting with Miguel was a clear transgression.

On the way Miguel briefly explained who we would meet when we got to his home: his mother and grandmother. His little sister, Iria, should also have been there, but some friends had come round and they'd gone swimming in the river. 'Just women, I'm the man of the house,' said Miguel jokingly. When I asked about his father, he explained he was in Bilbao, working as a foreman for a building company. He'd been away for more than five years; he was good at what he did and in the Basque Country not only did he have a permanent job, but the salary was a lot higher. He came back one weekend a month and whenever he had any holiday. A sacrificial life, but the only way to earn enough money for the family to make ends meet.

'Emigration, Clara; it's the only path open to us if we want to do anything more than survive. I suppose my turn will come too, in a few years.'

I kept my mouth shut. What was I going to say about a situation so different from my own? I was glad we soon reached our destination, since Miguel's house was not far from the manor. It was in a place which could be considered the end of one of the town's streets or the beginning of the road to Betanzos. There were two houses, in fact. The one on the main road was a traditional building with two floors and a roof which was clearly very old. The front door and shutters on the ground floor were closed, as if no one lived there, though the windows on the first floor were open, white curtains billowing in the breeze. Behind this house was another, again with two floors, which had recently been built, though the side walls still hadn't been plastered. The front of this house gave onto a track which left the main road and continued between allotments and meadows.

'What about this house?' I asked, seeing Miguel pass in

front of the old house and head towards the other. 'Who lives there?'

'Nobody. It used to belong to my great-grandfather Ishmael. Both my mother and grandmother were born there. My sister and I were born somewhere else; when my parents got married, they went to live in a rented flat near the main square. When they had Iria, they decided to build the new house behind; the land belonged to the family and my father built it little by little.'

'How long have you been living here?'

'We moved about four years ago. You can see it's still unfinished, but we don't have enough money for any more. We sometimes talk about doing up the old house, but we'd need to win the lottery for that.'

Miguel opened the white aluminium door and showed me into a hall where there were several pots with begonias. On the left was a staircase leading to the first floor, and on the right a double glass door which led to what looked like a sitting room. In front of us was a long corridor, at the end of which was another door, which was open and let in the bright light from outside.

A woman came in with a sack in her hand. As soon as she saw us, she put it down and came towards us, rubbing her hands on her apron. She looked older, she must have been about forty, and the hand she held out had the rough skin of people who are used to manual work. She smiled at me openly and, having introduced herself as Irene, Miguel's mother, showed me into the sitting room I'd seen, though they obviously didn't use it very often since everything in there was too ordered, like a stage set.

In the middle of the sitting room was an oblong table made of thick, dark wood. On top of it, on a lace cloth, was a crystal vase with a bunch of freshly cut roses. Around the table were six matching chairs with green velvet seats. There was also a matching cupboard against one of the walls, which struck me as very beautiful. My attention was drawn to a flowery sofa which looked very out of place next to all that old furniture. Finally, next to the window was a small cabinet with glass doors which revealed shelves full of books. Hanging on the wall, a reproduction of *Sunflowers* by Van Gogh and another of an Impressionist painting by Renoir, with some women walking through a field of poppies. I noticed the absence of a television, more evidence that this was not where the family lived.

Miguel steered me away from the sofa towards one of the dining chairs. Then, as if he'd read my thoughts, he said:

'The sofa was bought, but the rest of the furniture was made by my grandfather Xoán. He was a carpenter all his life, had his workshop here, on the same land where this house was built. They say he was very good at his profession, I bet you there's a piece or two of his furniture in the manor house.'

'Daddy died young, in the summer of 1978, he wasn't even sixty,' added Irene. 'He suffered a heart attack while carrying some planks and never recovered. The ambulance from Coruña took a long time and, when they reached the hospital, it was too late. This might not have happened today, things are a bit better, but then there weren't the same means.'

I remained quiet, I never knew what to say in such situations, and Miguel didn't seem willing to help me. Irene announced she would bring us coffee, everything was ready. When we were left alone, I said to Miguel:

'I'm happy to meet your mother, but the one we came to see was your grandmother. Where is she?'

'In the upstairs sitting room. We'll go up shortly, but first we have to drink the coffee Mum will serve us. If we don't, she'll be offended and I'll have to pay the consequences.' He gave me a conspiratorial look and added, 'Watch how she brings the new coffee set. You're an important visitor to her, you must be the first person from the manor to enter this house.'

'What about those books?' I asked, pointing to the cabinet.

'I was waiting for you to ask about them. They're my family's pride and joy: the books from the trunk, the inheritance left us by Ishmael, the few books which were saved from the flames.'

'And the trunk?' I asked stupidly.

'The trunk is up in the attic. We had to take them out, otherwise they'd have rotted.'

I walked over to the cabinet. They were all old books, most of them clothbound, with the titles engraved on the spine in letters which had once been golden. The dominant colours were blue and brown, though they'd faded through the passage of time.

I opened the glass doors and took out one of the volumes. The pages inside were yellow, especially around the edges, and the marks of dampness were obvious. I didn't pay attention to this, however, but to the titles I read at random, most of them in Spanish: *The Last of the Mohicans* by James Fenimore Cooper, *A Tale of Two Cities* by Charles Dickens, *The Captain's Daughter* by Alexander Pushkin, *Crime and Punishment* by Fyodor Dostoevsky, *Madame Bovary* by Gustave Flaubert, *The Mysterious Island* by Jules Verne, *The Mother* by Maxim Gorky, *The Gold-Bug* by Edgar Allan Poe... There was also a shelf with books by Galician authors whose names I recognized from my literature classes: *Circling* by Ramón Otero Pedrayo, *Things* by Alfonso Castelao, *In the Starry Night* by Ramón Cabanillas, *New Leaves* by Rosalía de Castro, *The Divine Sketch* by Manuel Curros Enríquez...

I was interrupted by Irene, who came in with a tray and placed it on the table. The coffee set, from Sargadelos, was brand new. When I saw it, I couldn't help smiling at Miguel.

'So you're Don Víctor's daughter, are you?' asked Irene, having served the coffee. 'When I was little, your father was a grown man. He must be seven or eight years older. He was very handsome, you've probably seen him in photos. Not surprising really: his father, Don Pablo, always carried himself very well, not to speak of Dona Rosalía, who, even before she died, despite her years, could still turn a few heads whenever she went out for a walk.'

As all I did was nod and smile, Irene added:

'But you've brothers, haven't you?'

'Yes, I have. Samuel and Rubén, both twelve. They're twins,' I answered.

Her questions looked every bit as if they would

continue for a long time, but Miguel came to my aid:

'That's enough, Mum, no more questioning. Next time Clara comes, she can tell you other things. But the person we're here to see today is Gran. Do you think she'll be awake?'

Irene apologized and quickly left, explaining she had work in the kitchen. We finished our coffee, went out of the sitting room and climbed the stairs. At the top was a corridor with a door at the end and two more on either side. Miguel led me down to the end and opened the door into another sitting room with a large window looking out onto the allotments behind. The furniture was new, with the excessive sheen of furniture when it's low quality. There was a TV stand, a sideboard, sofa and low table. In an armchair sat an old woman with a long face and deep wrinkles. Her eyes were like Miguel's or even bluer. She had white hair neatly combed back into a bun. She wore a grey blouse and a long, darker skirt. I had the impression she'd dressed up especially for me.

'Hello, Gran!' said Miguel happily. 'There's someone here wants to meet you.'

Then, turning to me, he added:

'Clara, this is my grandmother Hortensia. The daughter of my great-grandfather Ishmael, who I told you about the other day.'

After we'd kissed each other on the cheek and exchanged a few pleasantries, Hortensia stared at me for a while, examining the details on my face.

'You look just like your grandmother! I look at you and have the impression I'm seeing her as a young girl,' she said finally. 'Dona Rosalía was very, very pretty. And you're the same. Who'd have thought it, the way things turn out!'

I didn't know what to say and began to feel the visit had been a mistake. I was tired of hearing the members of my family always referred to as 'Don' or 'Dona'. To me they were just my parents and grandparents and I didn't like the way they treated them out of fear or respect. What did they call me? Miss Clara? And I wasn't there to be questioned, but to hear what Miguel had described to me, the memories of this old woman, memories which might shed light on my grandparents and a time I knew nothing about.

'Gran, Mum just gave Clara a grilling,' said Miguel, sensing my discomfort. 'Why don't you tell us what we talked about after the skeleton appeared?'

Hortensia smiled and glanced at me apologetically. She remained silent for a while, as if ordering the words she was about to say.

'You must have been quite taken aback the other day,' she began. 'Miguel told me you were there when they discovered the body in the storeroom.'

I quickly realized her words hid a question, perhaps this was her way of exercising her memories. I told her about everything which had happened that day, omitting to mention only the ring which I kept in my bedside table.

'So it's true there was a hole in its skull,' she remarked, having listened closely. 'I heard people say this, but thought it was just gossip, people are always coming up with stories.'

I remained quiet. It was her turn to talk now, if there was something she wanted to tell me. I had to be patient and wait for her to begin to unlock her memories.

'That man must have been there since the war, there's no other explanation,' she said, as if to herself. 'Ever since I found out, I haven't been able to get the images of those years out of my head, it's as if I had to relive it all. Can you believe that hadn't happened to me for quite some time? I always made an effort to forget, you just can't live with so much misfortune inside you. And now this corpse appears, like a gust of wind to set everything in motion. My head is full of memories and there's nothing I can do.'

She fell silent, gazing at the white clouds on the other side of the window. Then, as if returning from an imaginary journey, she looked at me and said:

'At my age, memories bring nothing but grief. The war was a very sad time, we were all overcome by sadness. So many people died who were not to blame! Some, like my brother Luís, managed to escape and avoid certain death. Others, like my father, who'd done nothing at all, spent several bitter years in prison and never recovered.

'That corpse you found has been keeping me awake. Every night I go back to the Vilarelle of that time, as in a film which returns me to my childhood. Besides my family, your grandmother Rosalía always appears at the heart of my memories. And Rafael, the boy she was in love with.'

'Rafael?' I interrupted her in surprise. 'Don't you mean Pablo? She married Pablo, my grandfather.'

'Don Pablo was in love with her, so was everybody, but at the time Rosalía didn't pay him much attention. She was crazy about Rafael, I should know. But war broke out and turned their lives upside down, as it did so many people's.'

As she talked, her voice grew slower and fainter, as if the memories she kept were reluctant to be transformed into words. After what she'd just said, I realized the conversation could be a lot more important than I'd thought. This woman was in possession of information which concerned me and I knew nothing about. The only image I had of Grandma Rosalía was that of the elderly lady I'd known as a child; of my grandfather, not even that. What could I say about when they were young, about the life they led back then? Nothing, or very little; only what I'd picked up at family meals, the odd anecdote which made no sense to me. The unexpected mention of this Rafael my grandmother had fallen in love with disturbed family certainties it had never occurred to me to question. A few days before I'd been confronted by a baffling mystery, and that afternoon chance – in the guise of an old woman I'd just met – had placed me in front of another.

7

'Are you in a hurry, Clara? What I'm going to tell you is long, we old people have lots of life stored up in our memories. But I don't want to bore you, mine are just stories about a remote past.'

Miguel's grandmother did not look like the same woman I'd met a little earlier. Her whole face was glowing, as if lit on the inside, and her eyes shone with an intensity which surprised me. I explained she shouldn't worry about me, I was there to listen to her stories, especially those which had something to do with Grandma Rosalía.

'It's a shame my father and my brother Luís aren't here. They'd tell it much better than me,' she remarked sadly. 'I was only little when the war started, barely thirteen. That was the end of my childhood, I was forced to mature quickly and endure misfortunes it's still painful to remember.'

'Miguel's told me a lot about your father. He said he was a bookbinder.'

'Yes, he was. A bookbinder by profession, a reader by vocation. One day you'll have to see the books of his we kept, the ones they didn't burn.'

'She already did, Gran,' said Miguel. 'We'll take a closer look when we go back down.'

'What about that brother you talked about?' I asked so she would continue.

'Luís was eleven years older than me. He had to escape at the end of the war, there was no other path open to him. In Mexico he started his life again, like other refugees. It was hard for us not to see him during all those years. For him too, obviously. He visited us after Franco died, but he never wanted to come back. He died in Mexico five years ago this autumn.'

'He came back in his own way,' Miguel interrupted her. 'He asked to be cremated and for his ashes to be scattered in the wood on the other side of the river. I sometimes go walking there, especially in the autumn. I like to think there's something of my uncle's ideals in the grass and dry leaves I step on as I walk.'

I glanced at Miguel, asking him with my look to be quiet. If I wanted to hear what this woman wished to tell me, we had to let her talk without interruptions.

'My brother and your grandfather were the same age. They had dealings with each other, they were both young men, I could even say they were friends before the war put paid to that,' continued Hortensia. 'When I was little, the lord of the manor was Don Raimundo, who I suppose would be your great-grandfather. After they had their first child, your great-grandmother couldn't get pregnant again, something to do with blood incompatibility. That child was Don Pablo, your grandfather. I still remember watching him pass in front of the house, by car or on horseback, as if he owned the world. It's not your fault, sweetheart, don't be offended, but the Soutelos were the local bosses, you couldn't move a leaf without their permission.'

'At home I've heard my grandmother's family was also rich,' I remarked uncomfortably.

'It was. The Bermúdez had lots of money, the father made a fortune in Cuba, but they didn't have the same prestige as the Soutelos. The house of the Cuban, as we called him in town, was nice, but nothing like the manor house. They had four children, all boys except for Rosalía. She was pretty, seemed from another world, always wearing elegant clothes, while we, you can imagine, spent the whole day dressed in rags.'

'Shall I tell her about the children in Africa, Gran?' Miguel interrupted.

'What children in Africa?' I asked in surprise, before Miguel's grandmother could reply.

'Not long ago, one evening we were watching a film on TV. It took place in an African country at the time Africa was being colonized by Europeans. In one scene the main characters, all of them white, were about to go on safari, looking elegant, clean, self-assured. Some local children stood at the roadside, covered with dirt, surrounded by clouds of flies. They looked at the whites in amazement, as if they were gods from another world who'd deigned to set foot on earth. And so Gran said, "That's exactly how we viewed the Cuban and manor families when we watched them go by."'

'My family was poor, we all were in Vilarelle,' continued Hortensia, slightly annoyed by the interruption. 'But my father had a wealth which set him apart: his profession, his love of books. If the manor still has a library, there'll be lots of books he bound. I suppose that's where he got his ideas from, he was one of the few people in town who dared to voice their sympathy for the Republic. My brother took after him, he also read everything he could lay hands on. Shame he couldn't study, there was nothing here back then. It was only when he was older, in Mexico, he became a lawyer. Such is life, there's nothing you can do, you have to take it as it comes.

'The greatest impact the Republic had was on education; even here, in Vilarelle, we noticed the change, despite being in the back of beyond. It was then they built the graded schools, where the social centre is now. And sent new teachers. Before that we'd only had a schoolmaster for boys and a schoolmistress for girls. And half the time we didn't even have class, they were often absent; ours was almost always ill, or so she said.

'The reason I'm telling you this is because Rafael was one of the new teachers, the only man, the other two were women. They arrived in the autumn of 1934, I remember it well. I was twelve then, it was my last year at school. Soon after term started, all the older girls were completely besotted with him. It was hardly surprising: he was easy to like, he was clever, pleasant, polite... And handsome, we couldn't take our eyes off him. We weren't used to seeing men around here walk with such bearing, such pride, as if they were equal in every way to those in the manor house.

'Some stories I heard from others, I already told you I was quite young. They're events I didn't understand until my father explained them to me in detail when he got out of prison. Rafael soon became great friends with Luís, and then with my father. It was normal, outside the manor there wasn't another house in town where people read so much as in ours. What's more, the three of them shared the same ideals. It was then Daddy and the teacher founded a cultural association. Rafael often came to visit, I remember many evenings he stayed for dinner. They talked about books for hours and also discussed politics. They didn't even notice me, I was always helping Mummy in the kitchen, but I found Rafael so handsome I did what I could not to miss a word of what he said.'

Everything this woman was telling me was interesting, but it wasn't what I wanted to hear, since she only referred to my family in passing. I must have gestured impatiently because she looked at me with those gleaming eyes of hers and went on:

'Your grandfather, as you well know, defended other ideas. Or other interests, if the two are ever somehow separated. But this didn't stop Rafael and Don Pablo becoming friends. I often saw them chatting in the bar or walking together down the road in front of our house.'

'Let me see if I understand you,' I remarked. 'You wish to tell me my grandfather and this teacher, Rafael, were friends? But didn't you say they had opposing ideas?'

'They did, but they were both young and cultured, they liked to talk. There weren't many people like that in Vilarelle; there was my brother, then Sebastián and the others who helped found the association. But they'd been born here and Don Pablo viewed them differently.'

'And didn't you say in my grandmother's family, the Cuban family as you call them, there were also three young sons?'

'Don't take offence, I know you're somehow related, but the Cuban boys were not the slightest bit interested in culture. They were interested in money and girls. I don't even want to think about the eldest, he was a bad man who did terrible things during the war. His name was Héctor, I don't know if they've ever talked about him at home. He was the leader of the Falangists, they say he decided who they were going to kill, and who not. The only one who was different in that house was your grandmother Rosalía, she must have taken after her mother.

'Rosalía was pretty and clever; as I said, there wasn't a single boy who wasn't in love with her. The normal thing would have been for her to marry Don Pablo, people in their position always end up together. But sometimes things turn out differently. And, don't ask me why, the one Rosalía fell head over heels in love with was Rafael.

'God forgive me, I don't mean to hurt anyone, but theirs was a crazy affair, so much so that Rosalía was determined to run away from home in order to marry him. My father told me about it many years later, he confessed he'd helped them to arrange secret meetings. My mother didn't approve of his actions, but even so some afternoons he closed his workshop so that the two of them could have some time together. He was also going to help them with their plans to leave, for Madrid or Paris; you may not be aware that back then a woman couldn't get married without her father's consent. The Cuban would never have accepted as his son-in-law a man he knew nothing about, with Republican ideas and not a penny to his name. Her brothers, especially Héctor, even less so.'

'But my grandmother ended up marrying my grandfather,' I objected, confused by what I'd heard. 'What happened then?'

'The war started, my girl, and put an end to everything which was good at that time. The wave of hate prompted by Franco's men reached even here, a small town like Vilarelle. It wasn't difficult for them to take control, self-declared Republicans were in the minority. That didn't stop them being brutal, lots of people turned up at the roadside with a bullet in their head. My father wasn't killed, but they ruined his life. All our lives, there are some things you just can't forget.'

Hortensia told me lots of stories that afternoon, it seemed the corpse in the manor house had opened the floodgates of her memory. When I asked her directly about my grandfather, all she said was that he'd been on the soldiers' side from the start. The Soutelos represented traditional power, they knew where their place was in that war. As for Héctor and my grandmother's other two brothers, Hortensia refused to go into detail, even though I kept on asking her. It was obvious, however, that they'd been responsible for a lot of the deaths and acts of revenge Vilarelle had seen.

Of all the people I heard about in her stories, I was most interested in this Rafael my grandmother was so besotted with. I couldn't help linking his name to the letter on the ring I'd found, though I knew it was a weak association, since there are lots of names beginning with 'R' and none of my fantasies fitted in with the answers Hortensia gave my persistent questions about the schoolteacher.

'Don Rafael? Daddy said he went into hiding for a few days, but then managed to cross the border with Portugal and take a boat to Argentina. After the war, from Mexico, my brother tried to find him, but failed. We never heard any more about him.'

When she saw the look of frustration on my face, she added:

'The one who might know something is Sebastián, he stayed in touch with the refugees.'

'Who's Sebastián?' I asked.

'A local lawyer, a bit younger than Luís. He retired a few years ago, I don't think he's very well.'

'If you'd like to talk to him, we can visit him at home one of these days,' said Miguel. 'I'm sure he'd receive us, wouldn't he, Gran?'

'Of course he would. You tell him you're my grandson and there won't be a problem.'

It was eight o'clock when I said goodbye, first to Miguel's grandmother and then to his mother. Miguel walked me back to the manor. On the way, I can't remember why, I mentioned how much I liked being alone in the mirador, having the sensation there was no one in the world but me.

'I like being alone too. It may seem strange, but it looks as if we have something in common,' remarked Miguel in the tone of irony I found so annoying.

I remained silent. I couldn't think of a suitably sarcastic reply, nor did I want to spoil that afternoon in which I'd discovered so many things in his company. As we were approaching the enclosure wall, Miguel said:

'Do you mind if I ask you a question?'

'Since when did you start asking for permission?' I replied, laughing. 'Especially from a member of the Soutelo family!'

'I'm being serious. Would you like to accompany me to Charming Rock? It's a special place, next to the river. It's where I go when I want to be alone. I'm sure you'd like it.'

'OK,' I answered straightaway. I was happy at the prospect of seeing Miguel again so soon. 'I might even get used to jumping over this wall.'

'This time you'll have to leave through the front gate since we'll be going by bike. It's quite far away, about four miles from here.'

'Well, I'm free almost any day. I can always say I'm going for a bike ride, I'm sure nobody would be surprised.'

'I can't tomorrow, I agreed to go to the garage in the afternoon. But perhaps the next day.'

'Whatever you decide. Just let me know beforehand. Though you'd better not call on the phone, that would make them ask questions at home. And I'm pretty sure my parents wouldn't agree to my going out with you.'

I was waiting for Miguel to say something sarcastic, but he kept quiet. We reached the part of the wall we'd jumped over and he helped me climb back into the estate. When I arrived at the house, I saw no one had noticed my absence. I told my mother I'd been reading in the mirador and she must have found it normal, because she didn't reply. It was a good excuse, one I could use when we went to see that Sebastián who might be able to tell me more about the mysterious Rafael who'd conquered my grandmother's heart.

8

Thanks to the detailed, impassioned notes I wrote in my diary every evening, I know my uncle Carlos arrived at the manor on the twenty-second of July. Carlos was my father's brother and a year younger than him; though there was a certain family likeness between them, that's where the similarities ended, since in their character and outlook on life they were like chalk and cheese. They treated each other with politeness, but it was easy to see a hidden coldness in their relationship.

Carlos got on very well with Mummy, they could spend hours discussing books and painters, which may have been why he came to share a few days of his holiday with us every summer. That year he planned to stay in the manor until mid-August. As he would confess to me later on, a return to Vilarelle meant something special to him, since the centre of the world is always somehow to be found in the places where we spent our childhood, where we experienced feelings and emotions which left a permanent mark.

Uncle Carlos had been living in Barcelona for years. He'd moved there after studying art history in Santiago and only ever returned to Galicia on short visits, when he tried to meet up with some of the painters who regularly exhibited in his galleries. Because over the years my uncle had achieved prominence in the artistic world in Barcelona; he owned three art galleries, one of them among the most prestigious in the city, and a small publishing house which specialized in art books with a low print run. Wonderful books, to tell the truth, rare jewels aimed at a select group of people who could afford such luxuries.

Although we kept up a regular correspondence, I hadn't seen him since Christmas, when he paid a flying visit to our house in Coruña. I was very happy to see him again. Carlos considered me his favourite niece and I had lots of reasons to return his affection. A few years later, when we no longer had any secrets between us, he would tell me he'd always seen in me the daughter he wanted but never had. As a child, what I appreciated most were the special gifts he brought me on every visit, my most beautiful toys were always from him. He also brought my brothers presents and no doubt he didn't forget Aunt María's children, but he always made it clear where his preferences lay. The fact they weren't just words became obvious that summer and especially during the last years of his life.

His name is also linked to my passion for books. I suppose it was my mother who made me an assiduous reader, if it's true what they say about reading being a vice someone has to give you. But I cannot overlook the important role Carlos played, since the few weeks every year we spent together I always remember him telling me stories (he'd read to me in bed those days, a ritual which gave us both great pleasure) or accompanying me on walks. Now that I think about it, he can't much have liked all that nonsense about the Famous Five and others like them I couldn't get enough of when I was nine or ten. But I would ask him to read these books and he would take the trouble to do so, which allowed him to share the things I enjoyed.

As I began to grow up, he seemed consciously to assume some of the responsibility for my education, even if it was at a distance, and started frequently sending me books which were always so well chosen it was as if they'd been written specifically for me. I owe him, more than anyone else, the passion for reading I've had since my teens, which I suppose will never leave me.

The previous summer we'd spent the months of July and August in a cottage my mother's family owned in Ombre, on the outskirts of Pontedeume, which remained empty for most of the year. Uncle Carlos came to spend a few days and, more than other summers, deliberately sought out my company, perhaps because he noticed I'd left my childhood behind and was beginning to experience the inner loneliness which overwhelms us in our teenage years. We'd often go on outings together, by bike or in his car, and I can say it was then our conversations moved onto a deeper level, creating bonds of trust between us which would never be broken.

I particularly remember one day we visited Eume Forest and decided to climb up to the ruins of Caaveiro Monastery. It was a weekday morning and we didn't meet another soul either during the difficult ascent or once we'd reached the top. The two of us were alone between the monastery's crumbling walls, gazing out at the wonders of nature: the two sides of the Eume valley, so steep it made you dizzy just to look at them, covered with trees which formed a compact mass of differing tones of green. At the bottom was the river, glistening like a motionless snake lying in the sun, though we both knew the impression was misleading, since we'd seen on our arrival how the waters rushed and tumbled along.

'I love this land deeply, with every year it hurts me more to leave it,' said Carlos. 'There's something in Galicia you only really appreciate when you're far away.'

'If you like it so much, why did you move to Barcelona?'

'Don't you know, Clara? I can't believe you're so naive, my clever niece can't be as blind as all that.'

I continued looking at him, unsure what he meant. I could tell from his expression it was something important, but I didn't know how to respond.

'Did you never wonder why I didn't get married? I'm certainly old enough if we adhere to the social norms.'

'Well, I'll ask you now,' I replied. 'Why didn't you get married?'

'The truth is I did. Almost sixteen years ago, just after you'd been born. My partner's name is Andreu, though officially he's only my best friend. You must have heard me talking about him.'

As the meaning behind his words slowly dawned on me, I realized I'd known this for quite some time, even if it was the kind of knowledge which lies dormant inside us, waiting for the right words to appear. The fact he told me this, letting me in on his secret, simply bound us together even more strongly, as we showed in the letters we wrote during the school year, which were very different from the innocent missives I'd sent him as a child. Now I confided in him as a teenager, a girl who was unsure of herself and eager to learn. I've often thought this was because I found in my uncle a tenderness and intimacy which my father lacked, he was always so distant, and my mother was unable to give me, since I was at a stage when I needed to distance myself from her and affirm my own identity.

Carlos arrived in the middle of the afternoon. He'd left Barcelona two days earlier, but stopped in Bilbao to see the work of some Basque painters he was interested in. He'd driven his car – a red Maserati the twins and my cousins greatly admired – all along the Cantabrian coast, a longer route but one he liked to take when he wasn't in a hurry.

After the kisses and other paraphernalia associated with a welcome, my uncle asked me to accompany him to his bedroom. He would stay in the one he'd occupied as a child, when he lived in the manor, and I saw how he became emotional when he went in and discovered all the furniture was more or less in the same place.

'It's strange how time alters our perception of things,' he remarked as if to himself. 'This room is large, you can see, but as a child it struck me as enormous. And cold! The winters here were cold, some years everything was covered with snow for days on end. They'd light the fires and put heaters and braziers in all the rooms, but the house is so big it was impossible to heat.'

I find it difficult to convey the joy I felt when listening to him, fascinated as I was by everything he said. The more I grew, the more I realized I wanted to appropriate his way of understanding life and being in the world. That afternoon I sensed my uncle could be the one to break the isolation manor life had forced me into, to help me overcome social rules I had no use for.

'Here are your presents,' Carlos opened one of his suitcases and produced two parcels. 'Or did you think I'd forgotten?'

I took the parcels and sat down in a chair so I could open them. I was amazed to discover what the smaller one contained; as always, Carlos had managed to find something which perfectly suited my tastes. He knew from my letters I'd become interested in music I hadn't paid attention to before. For months now, I'd been particularly drawn to the blues. So it was with emotion I examined what was in my hands: a four-CD set with a selection of the best blues recordings ever made, starting with the earliest by singers I'd never heard of and ending with musicians I'd just begun to know, like Muddy Waters or John Lee Hooker.

When I opened the second parcel, I found it contained two books: *Moon Palace* by Paul Auster and *A Portrait of the Artist as a Young Man* by James Joyce. I'd never heard of them, but the fact my uncle had chosen them was guarantee enough for me.

'I think you'll like them, especially Paul Auster,' he said. 'You're old enough to be reading stories which deal with life on a deeper level.'

'You always make a good choice. Once I've finished the book I'm reading, I'll get started on these.'

'What book is that?'

'*Brave New World* by Aldous Huxley,' I said proudly.

This wasn't a title he'd given me, but one I'd bought myself, intrigued by a passing comment my biology teacher had made when we'd been discussing cloning in class.

'Aldous Huxley! So you're into the Alpha Plus and poor Epsilon Minus. When I read it, years ago, the society he described seemed terrible; even more so now. I suppose when you look at it, all Huxley did was glimpse through a crack the future awaiting us. What he didn't do was imagine the drugs people would be given to live like slaves and carry on believing they were happy. That's somewhere fiction has been surpassed by the reality of today.'

I remained silent. The truth is I hadn't started it, I was still reading Dickens' novel, but I was spurred on to do so by Carlos' comments. I leafed through the books while my uncle put the clothes he'd brought in the wardrobe. At one particular moment, as if making a routine observation, he asked:

'So how's your love life?'

His question caught me by surprise. Or rather, what caught me by surprise was to find myself thinking about Miguel, as if an association had been established outside my control which I hadn't noticed before. I blushed in confusion and embarrassment. My uncle realized immediately:

'You've gone all red! Well, there must be something, you haven't learned yet to conceal your emotions. You'll have to tell me, this is a chapter I do not want to miss.'

When he saw I didn't say anything and it was all I could do to hide my embarrassment, he didn't insist. He carried on putting his clothes on the shelves while I calmed myself down. Having finished, he asked:

'So how are things here? Your dad's now lord of the manor, he's finally achieved it. He must be walking so tall he can't fit under the doors, around here that was always the highest distinction.' He adopted a theatrical pose and continued, 'The Soutelo family! This manor has always been important, like a castle in the Middle Ages. All it lacked was a ghost!'

'Well, it may not have a ghost, but it does have a skeleton. Did you know we discovered one soon after we arrived?'

'A skeleton? What are you talking about, Clara?'

Given my uncle's interest, I asked him to sit down next to me and proceeded to tell him everything I knew. Everything from the morning I was an accidental witness to the discovery in the small compartment between two walls to what I'd heard my parents say. Though the truth is I didn't tell him everything since I omitted to mention the ring and my fantastic hypotheses following what Miguel's grandmother had told me. I don't quite know why, since my relationship with my uncle was close enough; I didn't think it necessary and preferred to wait until later on.

'If there were two bullets, that person must have been murdered,' said Carlos, having listened to me with rapt attention. 'Did no one claim the body? Do they know how long it's been there?'

'Daddy can fill you in on the details. All I know is the judge came, and the Civil Guard, and Daddy had to go to the courthouse, he was pretty annoyed. As for the rest, you'd better ask him.'

My uncle broached the subject with my father on the same day, after dinner. Alfredo and the twins had just left the table and gone to watch TV. Ana and I remained sitting, I suppose we felt we had the right to partake in some of the adults' rituals.

'Clara told me about the skeleton you found during the building work. That must have been quite a surprise!' my uncle began. Then, addressing Daddy directly, he went on, 'Tell me something about it, Víctor, you must know more about what happened.'

My father tried to cover up his initial confusion, though it wasn't difficult to see, and exchanged a fleeting glance with my mother. They both seemed to be made uneasy by Carlos' comments.

'A most regrettable incident,' my father finally brought himself to say. 'Not only did it postpone the building work for several days, it caused several problems, especially to me. I had to make a statement, fill out forms... that kind of thing.'

'And Víctor did his best to control the journalists,' Mummy intervened. 'It was reported on the first day in the odd newspaper, but after that it disappeared. And wasn't even mentioned on the radio or television.'

'It wasn't easy,' my father boasted. 'I had to use all my influence to stop them bothering us, otherwise it could have turned into an unpleasant scandal for us and the family name.'

'But don't they know anything about the deceased? Hasn't he been identified, hasn't anyone expressed an interest in him? What are they saying in town?' Carlos seemed unwilling to let my father brush the matter aside.

'No doubt they've come up with all kinds of stories in town, you know what people are like. No, nobody's claimed the body. And if he did have relatives, I'm sure they'd all be dead by now.'

'All the same, as I understand it, the coroner has to file a report. And the courts have to open an official investigation,' insisted my uncle. 'Isn't that so?'

'It is, you're absolutely right.' Daddy produced one of the thin cigars he used to smoke after dinner and took his time lighting it. He clearly wasn't amused by Carlos' insistence. 'The coroner – she's a woman, you'll find them occupying any post these days – prepared a draft prior to her final report. There's nothing surprising in it, I'm sure you know two bullets were found with the remains.'

'Does she say how long the body had been there?'

'She calculates more than fifty years. So it could be from the Civil War or the forties. Those were troubled times, I don't think there's any way we can be certain.'

'I suppose so, if that's what the coroner says. I'm most intrigued by the two bullets, which clearly indicate the person was murdered,' my uncle would not let go of the bait. 'Has it occurred to you the murderer might be someone from the manor?'

'The murderer! Don't exaggerate! The corpse was found in the store, so it could have been anyone with access to that part of the building. One of the servants or those working on the land. Or an outsider, how should I know? Remember what Daddy always said, our grandparents spent a long period in Santiago, they didn't want to be here while there were still problems with fugitives,' my father had raised his voice, but he stopped when he realized and began speaking calmly. 'So it could have been anyone. Whoever wanted to conceal the crime chose the ideal place, no one would have thought to search in the manor house.'

'And aren't the courts going to do anything? I thought there were certain procedures...'

'There are and they've opened proceedings. But I've spoken to the judge, whose father is Alberto Riquer, a colleague of mine from Ferrol. He said the file will remain open but, if no one claims the body, no action will be taken. Bear in mind, even if we do find out who the remains belong to and who killed him, the facts occurred more than forty years ago. Legally the case has prescribed. So there isn't much point digging around.'

Hearing my father give out this information unsettled me. He knew all about it, the coroner's report, the court proceedings. If my uncle hadn't asked, he never would have mentioned it. Perhaps because I'd been the first person in the family to discover that corpse, I felt I had the right to know everything concerning it. But all my father was worried about was the Soutelos' good name, he clearly wanted to put an end to the subject.

Maybe he already had, but I had the ring and, since my conversation with Hortensia, I felt like pulling on threads which might help me to discover more. My uncle Carlos could turn out to be a useful ally; if there was someone I could trust, it was him. So when he caught my eye, I made a gesture he understood immediately. He changed the topic of conversation and began talking to my mother about the exhibition which had recently opened in Barcelona's Museum of Contemporary Art, a thorough examination of Russian avant-garde painting from the start of the twentieth century.

My mother saw her chance, there was nothing she liked more than having Carlos there to discuss painting. When a little later I left the table, the two of them were deep in conversation while my father smoked his cigar and listened to them without paying attention to a subject which I knew did not interest him.

I had made up my mind. I had to talk to Carlos and share with him everything Hortensia had told me. Though that would mean telling him as well about my relationship with Miguel – a relationship, I had to admit, I was beginning to consider very important.

9

Two days later, when I reached the mirador at about midday, on a corner of the bench I found a note from Miguel held down with a stone. He'd probably jumped over the wall first thing in the morning, on his way to work, knowing I went there almost every day. I can reproduce the whole text here, since I still have the folded piece of paper I later reread many times in the pages of my diary:

Can you come to the river this afternoon? If you can, I'll wait for you at four o'clock by the wall where we jumped over the other day. If you feel like swimming, there's a great place where we're going. If you can't come, don't worry, we'll go another time.

Miguel.

There was no way I was going to miss that meeting. After lunch I casually remarked that I might go for a bike ride, since I was convinced Ana wouldn't want to come. My uncle Carlos was the only one who talked about accompanying me, but I said I'd prefer to go on my own and he didn't insist.

I left the manor at four, on my bike, with a rucksack in which I'd put a towel and a bottle of water. Miguel was waiting for me with his bike in the place we'd arranged. Shortly after that, we were pedalling along side by side, since there were hardly any cars. I thought we'd follow the path to the river beach, but I was wrong. We went in the opposite direction, upstream, along a road which ran parallel to the river, but slightly higher up.

Having pedalled for more than half an hour, we reached a track which left the road and headed down to the river. Not only was it narrow, but it became thicker with vegetation the further down we got. I was sorry I'd worn shorts since, though we only had to pass through ferns and tall grass, it was dry grass which scratched my legs. A little before the river, the track opened out into a place where the grass was green and shorter, no doubt because of the shade from the alders growing on the riverbank. We left our bikes there, against the trunk of a tree, and followed a path which led between the alders, alongside the river.

We hadn't gone thirty yards when we reached the most amazing spot. The trees left the riverbank and opened out into a semicircle, surrounding a large central rock, a slab of stone which seemed to emerge from the ground and continue before sinking into the river, like the petrified back of some prehistoric animal. The riverbed here was wider and the water was deeper and so clear you could easily see the stones at the bottom. The branches of the alders, which protected the place from sight, cast shadows only on a part of the clearing, leaving most of the rock in sun.

'What did I tell you? Isn't it a magnificent place?' Miguel was obviously pleased by my reaction. 'My dad told me lots of people used to swim here but, after they made the river beach, they stopped coming.'

'You're right, it's almost magical,' I agreed, amazed by the sense of isolation. 'The mirador in the manor's pretty good, but this place is even better.'

'You don't know how relaxing it is to be here. I sometimes feel like I'm out of the world, as lonely as Crusoe on his island. I bring a towel and a book, and I don't leave till it's dark. Shame the summer here lasts so little.'

Before I continue writing, I must confess it's extremely easy for me to describe what happened that afternoon by the river because in the evening, carried by a sense of joy I'd rarely experienced, I filled six pages of my diary, going into minute detail about my feelings and emotions. I read them again now and I can't help being overwhelmed by nostalgic tenderness, perhaps because the words remind me of the passionate, innocent girl I was then. It's true that they're not very well written and I'm ashamed of the succession of adjectives ('unforgettable', 'magical', 'intense', 'wonderful', 'supreme'...) and clichés I used; but it's also true they retain some of the enthusiasm and passion for life which brought them about, causing me to re-experience some of the physical sensations I felt that afternoon for the first time.

I remember we got out our towels and placed them in such a way that we could sit on the grass and lean against the rock. Though we had planned to go swimming, I was suddenly ashamed by the idea of wearing a swimsuit there, on my own, with Miguel. I'd put on the red bikini I used to wear, but didn't dare take off my polo shirt or shorts.

Miguel must have felt something similar because he also sat down next to me in his clothes. It was fantastic being there, listening to the monotonous sound of the water, being caressed by the sun's rays from above.

'It's the first time I've come here with someone, till now I'd always come on my own. The books I've read, leaning against this rock!'

'I find it strange you like reading so much. I'd never have guessed it if you hadn't told me.'

I regretted the words as soon as they'd come out of my mouth. Miguel's response was immediate:

'Oh really? And why is it so strange? Because I come from a working-class family and have oil-stained hands?' His voice had regained the aggressive tone of our first meetings.

'I'm sorry, that's not what I meant. I meant because you're a boy. None of the boys in my class ever liked reading. And my brothers are as frightened of books as vampires are of garlic.'

I was trying to make amends, but the truth is Miguel's words had revealed the prejudice in me, a prejudice I was only aware of when I heard him say it. Luckily he seemed to accept my explanation and his features softened.

'Deep down I know you're right. It's not normal for there to be books in a house like mine,' the anger had disappeared from his voice. 'You heard what my grandmother said. Were it not for my great-grandfather Ishmael, I'd be like the other boys in town. But he passed on his enthusiasm to his children; and my grandmother passed it on to my mother.'

'Does your mother also read?'

'My mother works hard all day long, but she never goes to sleep without first reading a bit of her current novel. They're the two who passed it on to me. If my great-grandfather's ghost were roaming about the house, I'm sure it'd be pleased to have had such a positive influence.'

I fell silent, relieved to have made up for my earlier comment. I closed my eyes and succumbed to the sense of ease I felt in that place. The grass gave off that intense scent it only has in summer and the breeze gently stirred the leaves. It was Miguel who, a little later, picked up the conversation:

'You might find it strange I read. But there's something I find a lot stranger.'

'What's that?'

'That we should be here together. You're from the manor house, part of the group of holidaymakers who come here to show off in front of those from the town. Who am I? A boy whose dreams are crushed by reality, no more, no less.'

'You're not going to talk to me about class differences again, are you?'

'No, it's simpler than that. The truth is I hated all of you. I couldn't bear seeing you so elegant, so happy, so unconcerned by anything except having fun. Always passing us by as if we were invisible.'

'What do you have against us? Against me?' I protested. 'This is the first summer I'm aware of being here, the others I was just a girl who went where she was taken.'

'Don't get me wrong, Clara. I've nothing against you, I wouldn't be here with you if I did. But I can't help feeling anger towards you all. That air of superiority the rich have, the security of knowing life will always go by without too many problems. While the rest of us have to scrape a living, here or outside, like my dad.'

'But it's not my fault I was born into my family,' I complained. 'I'm not saying you're not right about some things; these days I had no choice but to be with some of your so-called holidaymakers and they struck me as pretty ridiculous.'

'And I don't?'

Instead of replying, I leaned over towards Miguel and kissed him near the lips. He gave me an intense look which totally disarmed me, as if he were invading my inside. I blushed uncontrollably, having just remembered my reaction when my uncle asked about my love life. I don't know what Miguel was thinking because he immediately stood up and said:

'Let's go for a swim, now's the best moment. If we wait any longer, we won't have time to get dry.'

Miguel had lost his sense of shame and stripped down to his swimsuit. I was impressed by his strong, slender body which radiated vitality. He was tanned, though it was his face and arms which were really dark. I thought he'd slip into the water at the river's edge, but what he did was climb the rock and dive in. He made a perfect arc and then emerged a few yards away. He swam over to where I was; as he did so, his muscles rippled and I found him intensely attractive.

'What? Aren't you coming in?' he asked from the middle of the current. 'It's pretty deep, but you can touch the bottom.'

I put aside my modesty and removed my polo shirt and shorts. Then I entered the water, though I didn't dare to dive off the rock. As soon as I was in, I thought I'd die from the cold. The water was freezing. I gave a few nervous strokes to see if my body would react; the cold abated a little, but was still unbearable.

'I'm getting out right now! It's freezing, I don't know how you can stand it!' I said in a trembling voice.

'Go to the right of the rock, there's a kind of staircase,' Miguel suggested. 'If you hold onto that branch over there, you'll get out without a problem.'

I did what he said and was finally out of the water. I found my towel and quickly wrapped myself in it as the heat of the sun began to relieve the intense feeling of cold which had got down to my bones.

When Miguel came out a little later, I was still wrapped in my towel. It was then he came over and started rubbing me through the towel in an attempt to make me warmer. It was the first time I'd felt him so close. And the first time, when I dropped the towel, I'd felt his hands on my skin. There he was, in front of me, rubbing my arms and shoulders to make the cold go away while I noticed another kind of heat, a deeper heat, taking control of me. I was the one who put his arms around me. And although Miguel carried on stroking my back, he soon gave up doing this and embraced me with the same intensity with which my body drew close to his. I looked up at him and it was then we kissed. I've already said I can't bear all the adjectives I used in my diary, but I can understand the emotion I felt that day. I'd been kissed before, by boys from school, but this was different, the first kiss to leave an indelible mark on my memory. The two of us were trembling, and not from the cold; I later learned that, though Miguel had been out with other girls, for him too this was the first kiss where there was something more than simple physical desire.

Now, as I try to put into words something which is so alive in my memory, I can't help thinking of a film I saw a few months ago, *Hearts in Atlantis* directed by Scott Hicks, where there's a scene which reflects my feelings very well. In this scene Anthony Hopkins plays the role of a mysterious man who's come to live in the apartment above that of the main character, a boy who's leaving childhood. Having seen the look of fondness with which the boy says goodbye to his best friend, a charming girl, Hopkins asks if he would like to kiss her. The boy pretends to be disgusted and says no, there's no way. And then Hopkins eyes him as only he can and says, 'You will kiss her. It will be the kiss by which all others in your life will be measured.' This is what happened to me, that afternoon's kiss is like a shadow I will always carry on my lips.

We then lay on the ground, on Miguel's towel. And there we carried on kissing, in a close embrace, his hands exploring parts of my body only I had touched before then, while I experienced a flood of new sensations, so intense it still excites me to think of them today.

At some point we must have stopped kissing, perhaps because the sun, as it changed position, cast where we were into shade and the fresh breeze brought us back to reality. I'm not sure what we did next, some details I must have gone through under the influence of the sensations I'd just experienced. I can see myself going up the track to the road, wheeling my bike, and on the road going back to the town, both of us happy because of what had happened. But, as I said, these memories are distorted by the emotion of what went before.

As we were nearing the town, I asked Miguel if we could stop for a moment, since I had something to tell him. He looked at me in surprise; he must have thought it had something to do with what had happened at the river. But all I wanted was to share with him the secret I'd kept to myself. I felt so close to Miguel at that moment I wanted him to know everything about my life.

'There's something I didn't tell you when I described how we unearthed the skeleton. I found a ring that day, a silver ring which must have belonged to the deceased. One of those rings with a letter engraved on the top, you must have seen them.'

We were sitting in a small field next to the road. He looked at me in confusion, I suppose this was the last thing he expected to hear. As he remained quiet, I added:

'And do you know what letter was on the ring? The letter "R".'

'"R" for Rosalía. Or Rafael,' said Miguel, as if he'd read my thoughts.

We gazed at each other in silence, there are times when words are absolutely unnecessary. And then we kissed again eagerly, as if we were afraid in the coming hours the taste on our lips would fade.

'I think we need to talk to Sebastián, just as Gran suggested,' said Miguel after a while. 'I'll give him a call tomorrow and ask if we can see him. And we can go the first afternoon you're free.'

It was getting dark by the time we reached the manor. We said goodbye in front of the iron gate, I didn't want to have to give explanations if I was seen with Miguel. I waited in front of the door, watching him leave on his way home. Then I entered the manor house, joy filling my heart. I suppose I must have run up to my room and shut myself away before filling the pages of my diary with an excited account of the afternoon. An afternoon which, as I relive it after so many years, makes me feel both melancholy and exalted. As well as reminding me with a certain envy of the Clara I was that summer, when I was sixteen.

10

The following morning I had to reject my cousin Ana's repeated invitations to go with her to the casino club where the holidaymakers' children met in town. I never particularly felt like hanging out with that crowd, but I liked the idea even less after learning Miguel's opinion of them. I pretended I had a terrible headache and, when Ana left, I took the copy of *Moon Palace* my uncle had given me and headed for the mirador on the other side of the wood. I could be calm there, read or think about the hours I'd spent with Miguel, which were so imprinted in my mind, without worrying about being disturbed until it was lunchtime.

What I didn't expect was for my uncle Carlos to interrupt me. He turned up after I'd been absorbed in my reading for quite some time.

'Well, well, well! So this is where you keep hiding?' his voice made me jump, I hadn't heard him approach. 'I see I'm not the only one looking for a bit of solitude.'

'I feel well here, it's the part of the manor I like best,' I replied. I was happy to see him, perhaps because I needed to talk to someone who could understand the huge joy I felt inside. 'It's like being on a desert island, far away from everyone and everything.'

I don't know if my uncle turned up in the mirador by

chance or if he deliberately sought out my company. I remember he sat down next to me and we started discussing the novel. It was the first book by Paul Auster I'd read, I still didn't know back then he would become one of my essential writers, and I was impressed by the narrator's passion for life, a passion which matched what I myself was feeling that morning. We'd been talking about other authors and books for some time when Carlos abruptly changed the subject, as if he'd been waiting all along for the right moment to do so.

'And what do you think about what happened the other day at dinner?'

'What do you mean?'

'I mean your father's reaction when I asked him about the skeleton you found. He seemed very reluctant to discuss the matter, as if he preferred to believe nothing had happened.'

'Daddy says there's no point going over events from years ago,' I answered, unsure where my uncle was heading.

'Well, I think the opposite. I know it's not very nice to find out there was a tomb in the house for so long, but I think it's only natural to want to know who this unwilling guest was. Especially if he was murdered with a bullet in the head.'

'As far as I'm aware, my parents are concerned it might sully the family name,' I remarked. I realized I wasn't being entirely honest with Carlos, the logical thing would have been to tell him all my thoughts, but I preferred to hear what he had to say first.

'Well, I'd like to find out more details, I can't overlook

the fact I grew up here in the company of that corpse. I happen to be a Soutelo as well, I can't just erase the past. Nor do I want to, nobody chooses the family they're born into.'

'What makes you say that?' A shiver had gone down my spine when I heard my uncle's words, they were the same I'd said to Miguel during one of our first meetings.

'I'm a Soutelo. But I'm also Carlos and I have my own ideas. I took the decision years ago to renounce the family pride my father held so dear.' Carlos wasn't looking at me, he had his gaze fixed on the distant hills. 'As he would say if he were here, I was always a rebel. From his point of view, he was probably right. I suppose I was also influenced by feeling different, I may have used my homosexuality to broaden my horizons.'

'Is that why you moved to Barcelona?'

'That was the main reason. I couldn't breathe here; had I stayed in Galicia, I'd have gone crazy. Barcelona at the time was a place where I could live freely.'

'What were the other reasons?'

My uncle hesitated a little, as if he hadn't quite understood the question. I had to remind him he'd said that was the main reason, which clearly pointed to there being others.

'Yes, there were other reasons, but I remember most the one my mother gave me,' Carlos caught my eye and smiled sadly. 'I'd just graduated from Santiago University. That summer, back in the manor house, I felt lost, I wasn't sure what to do with my life. One day, when we were alone, Mummy spoke to me in a serious tone she'd never used before and told me to leave, to get away from here, from the family. She said I was different and, if I stayed, the shadow of the Soutelos would smother me and make me the same as my brother and sister, as everybody else.'

We both fell silent. My uncle often used to talk to me, I've already said I was his favourite niece, but I'd never felt him so close before. There I was, hearing intimacies which pointed to a significant change in our relationship, as if Carlos felt I was now mature enough for him to speak openly to me.

'I also left because of my father,' he continued after some time. 'He died many years ago, I suppose he should represent a closed chapter in my life. I loved him, it's true, but I also grew to hate him deeply and persistently. He may have been disappointed in me, Víctor was always his favourite. And María, well, she was a daddy's girl. But I was strange, I didn't fit in, he may have thought I wasn't worthy of the family name. And besides, I couldn't bear the way he was with my mother, she didn't deserve such treatment.'

'I barely know anything about my grandparents,' I remarked, surprised by what Carlos had said. 'I remember Grandma Rosalía of course, I was fourteen when she died. But I was only a few months old when Grandpa died, I only know him from a few photos in the manor house.'

'Daddy? He was the typical kind of local boss, there's no point denying it. When war broke out, he was on the side of Franco's soldiers from the start. What else was he going to do? He had to defend his interests. And boy, did they reward him for it: town mayor, provincial governor... I never asked him about his business, he was just one of many who grew rich under Franco's dictatorship.'

Carlos looked at me, as if he expected me to say something. But I had nothing to say, it was the first time I'd heard so much about my family. A moment later, my uncle added:

'I can understand all that, the dictatorship allowed a small minority to flourish. What I can't accept is the way he treated my mother, always with repressed anger and harsh silences, as if he had something against her.'

'Grandma and Grandpa got on badly?' I asked. 'Daddy never said anything, nor did Aunt María.'

'Everyone remembers what they want to, it's what they call selective memory. Victor always admired Daddy. But I was very close to my mother.'

'Why did Grandma put up with it?'

'For our sakes, I suppose, for her children. She was really sick of all his contempt, she told me so on several occasions. In fact she improved a lot after Daddy died. She seemed to revive, to become young again. They say this happens to lots of widows, but the change in her was spectacular.'

'Why didn't she get a divorce?'

'Those were other times, she had no choice. There would have been a huge scandal, especially among people of her class. Today it would have been different, she could have taken another decision and no one would have minded. After all, money wasn't an issue, with what she'd inherited she had more than she could use.'

My uncle carried on talking, more to himself perhaps than to me. I listened, amazed by the new world I was discovering. When my grandparents came up in conversation, my father only ever had commonplaces to say. I felt for the first time someone was showing me aspects of my family which could alter my view of them and were somehow related to what Hortensia had told me in Miguel's house a few days before.

'I also have to tell you something no one else knows,' I said to my uncle after a period of silence. I felt the time had come to repay his sincerity. 'Well, Miguel knows, but no one else.'

'Miguel? Who's Miguel?'

'You don't know him, he's a boy from the town I've recently become friends with.'

I suddenly blushed, I couldn't help it. I was very annoyed. My uncle must have noticed, but he kept quiet and stared at me with a look of interest.

'I went to his house the other day,' I continued. 'His grandmother knows lots of stories about the Civil War. And she told me things about Grandma Rosalía maybe even you don't know.'

I proceeded to explain all that chance had revealed to me during those July weeks. The discovery of the ring the morning we found the skeleton, my meetings with Miguel, the visit to Hortensia. The news about Grandma Rosalía's love affair with Rafael, the teacher who'd come to town during the Republic... My uncertainty, and that of Miguel, about the names which coincided with the letter engraved on the ring.

When I finished, my uncle didn't speak for a long time. It was as if my revelations had moved some of the pieces he kept in his head, making them fit together differently.

'I'm amazed!' he said finally. 'It's true children never know everything about their parents, but I can't help feeling bitter this Hortensia knew more about my mother than I ever did. I want to learn more details. I'm a lot more interested than you might think. So I'll have to rely on your investigative powers.'

'Miguel's too. He's the one helping me.'

'And those of this Miguel who seems so important to you. You'll have to introduce him to me one of these days,' added Carlos. 'I'm glad it was you who found the ring, and that you kept it a secret. If your father found out, he'd confiscate it immediately. In the same way he did the remains of that poor man who was murdered.'

'I don't think we'll ever know who it was,' I remarked sadly.

'Don't be so sure, Clara, my dear. I don't suppose you want another member in your team, three can be a crowd, but I can always help you from the outside. I too want to learn more about what happened. To start with, tomorrow I'll try to make contact with the coroner. I'm still a Soutelo after all. And around these parts that always opened a lot of doors.'

11

I continued seeing Miguel over the following days, though not every single afternoon. I always pretended I was going for a bike ride; Miguel would wait for me outside the manor, next to a small chapel on the road towards his house. Then we'd go far from the town, always somewhere different. With him I discovered a large part of the area around Vilarelle and visited places I would never have gone to with the holidaymakers.

We had a tacit agreement not to be seen together in town. I didn't want to bump into someone who might know me and go and tell my family. And Miguel, though he never actually said this, probably didn't want to be seen with me by his friends. So what we had became a kind of secret relationship in which, I now think, both of us were aware we were breaking the unwritten rules which governed our respective worlds.

On one such afternoon Miguel told me we would finally be able to pay Sebastián a visit. He'd tried arranging a meeting after the day we spoke to his grandmother Hortensia, but the niece who looked after him had said he wasn't well and she would let us know when he recovered.

'So he's expecting us tomorrow at five,' finished Miguel. 'His house is on the far side of the square, next to a small street which ends in a track, you can't miss it. I'll be waiting for you outside. Do you think you can make it?'

'If there isn't some disaster in the manor house, I'm sure I can,' I replied. 'Nobody will mind me going to town at that time. The only danger is Ana might want to tag along, but she's more to gain from leaving me alone.'

I reached the square the next day a little before five. Since Miguel hadn't appeared, I sat down on a stone bench and gazed at the house we were going to visit. It must once have been one of the most important houses in Vilarelle; though they were all very similar, this one stood out because of its size, it was almost twice as big as those around it. It was also the only one which had a front garden – if 'garden' is the right word for a small, fenced-off area with rosebushes and a few dahlias weighed down with crimson flowers.

It wasn't a tall building, none of them was. As well as the ground and first floors, it must have had a second floor beneath the hipped roof, since there was a large dormer window on each side. The most impressive feature at the front was the two balconies, their iron railings half hidden by the flowers growing in pots on the ground or attached to the balusters.

I was struck by how deep the building was and went down the side street Miguel had mentioned. It was obvious the back of the house was more important. There was a gallery lit by the afternoon sun, a wonderful vantage point where I felt there was someone looking at me from behind the windows.

As I returned to the bench, I was overjoyed to see Miguel entering the square. He wore that serious expression I knew so well, though the gleam in his eyes revealed that he too was pleased to see me. If I was expecting a token of affection on his part, I was disappointed, he didn't dare show it. With a glance he led me to understand there might be more than one pair of eyes peeping out at us from behind the curtains.

We went through the garden and rang at the door. It was opened by a slim woman with short, dark hair, aged about forty. She introduced herself as Carme and greeted me coldly. But not Miguel, whom she must have known, since they chatted away comfortably.

'Uncle's in the back gallery. Go upstairs and down to the end of the corridor. You can't get lost.'

Following her instructions, we climbed the stairs to the first floor. At the end of the corridor was a sitting room which opened out into the spacious gallery I'd spotted from outside. All the way along the room was a row of pots with plants, in particular brightly coloured begonias. The view from the gallery was amazing. You could see the breadth of the valley and the mountains on the horizon, crowned by what looked like an unending line of crosses but were actually wind turbines. A Calvary stretching off into the distance.

In a corner of the room, shielded from direct sunlight, an elderly gentleman sat in a tall-back armchair. He was very slight and had white, combed-back hair. Behind his tortoiseshell glasses a pair of bright, inquisitive eyes formed a sharp contrast to the pale colour of his skin.

'So you're Hortensia's grandson,' he said to Miguel after the initial greetings. We were both sitting opposite him.

'Though I should say Ishmael's great-grandson. What a man, your great-grandfather! There were few men like him, you're lucky if you've inherited some of his enthusiasm.'

The fact that Sebastián addressed only Miguel made me feel uncomfortable, as if I were somehow in the way, but I was wrong. Having asked after his grandmother and mother, he turned to me. The gleam in his eyes seemed to intensify when he said:

'So you're Clara. You know there's no need to tell me you're Rosalía's granddaughter. Her face is in yours, you're very similar. When you came in, I thought for a moment I was seeing Rosalía when she was young. She was very pretty, your grandma. We were all besotted with her.'

The woman who'd opened the door then entered the room, carrying a tray with a coffee set and a plate of assorted biscuits. She served coffee for Miguel and me, but in Sebastián's cup she put a spoonful of powder from a jar and filled it with milk.

'How I'd love to have a strong cup of coffee!' exclaimed Sebastián after the woman had left. 'But the doctor's forbidden it, so here I am, drinking instant chicory. Chicory, as in the famine years!'

We drank our coffee, nibbled some biscuits, exchanged a few pleasantries about town life... I started getting nervous and decided to cut to the reason we were there.

'Hortensia told us lots about before the war, when she was a girl. She also told us you were the one who'd know more. That's why we're here.'

'Hortensia was right. My heart and legs aren't what they used to be, but my head's still all right,' he had an open expression, as if he were pleased by our visit. 'This head of ours is a mystery. The older I get, the more I remember from my youth. So what do you want me to tell you?'

'I'd like to know more about my grandmother Rosalía,' I said immediately. It was true that I wanted to know more about her life, but I also wanted to know other facts, especially having listened to Hortensia's stories. As if he'd read my mind, Sebastián answered:

'I can tell you lots about Rosalía, we were good friends, but first I'd have to tell you things about me and other people who were around at that time.'

This had the appearance of a tennis match, it was obvious it would take ages to get to where I wanted, so I decided to be more direct.

'Hortensia mentioned my grandmother had a boyfriend, a schoolteacher named Rafael. Why don't you start with him?'

Sebastián seemed to hesitate. He may have been wondering whether it was a good idea to share his memories with two young people he'd just met. Or, it suddenly occurred to me, perhaps he didn't trust me because I was a Soutelo.

'Your grandma was very pretty, I already told you that,' he finally began. 'I knew her from the time she was a girl, but I'd better head straight to our adolescent years, before war broke out and our lives were ruined.

'Let me start by talking about myself, it will help you understand better what follows. My father was a lawyer, this gave him a position which made ours one of the town's few respectable families. Not like the Soutelos, of course;

the manor family was always a cut above the others, they'd been lords of the manor for years. I was sent to a boarding school in Coruña, from where I would return to Vilarelle at weekends. Then I went to study law in Santiago, since my father wanted me to take over the family firm.

'At the age of sixteen, I became very good friends with Luís, Hortensia's brother. Luís hadn't been able to study, back then this option was open to a small minority. In fact the only two people from town who went to university were your grandpa Pablo and me. But Luís read everything he could lay his hands on and became an expert in many fields, we could spend hours discussing politics or literature. I met Ishmael through him, the most fascinating person I ever came across. A true Renaissance man, he had a passion to learn about everything. He was a Republican and a Galicianist, in 1920 he founded Vilarelle's first Brotherhood of Language. Luís and I shared his ideals. In Santiago I'd met some extraordinary people, a whole generation of poets and painters who wanted to change the world. It was a time of great enthusiasm, when everything seemed possible, I'm not sure if you can understand.'

Everything Sebastián was telling us was interesting, especially for Miguel, who was hearing things about two of the most important members of his family. But it sounded to me like a history lesson, something I found difficult to tie in with the few details in my possession. I had to wait for this man to cover subjects I was interested in. My patience soon paid off as his conversation veered towards areas where I wanted to be.

'I'd like to talk about the summer of 1935, the last which deserves to be remembered with the joy we traditionally associate with that season. The following summer was wartime, when blood and hatred took over everything. It was that summer I met Rafael. He was a few years older than us, he must have been about twenty-five. He'd recently become friends with Luís, so it was inevitable we should meet.

'In fact, as I found out later, the person Rafael had a deeper relationship with was Ishmael. Despite the difference in age, they shared political ideals and a passion for books. They were the two who pushed for a branch of the Galicianist Party to be formed in Vilarelle. There weren't many of us in it, there can't have been fifteen. I say "us" because Luís and I were also members. A bunch of idealists, an island in a sea of ignorance. The elections of February 1936 were won by the right, those of us in the Popular Front didn't even get two hundred votes.'

'What does all this have to do with my grandmother?' I asked impatiently.

'Patience, Clara, everything in its time. If I don't tell you this, you won't understand what comes next, when your grandma Rosalía enters the scene. She'd be about eighteen, the prettiest girl I'd ever set eyes on. Clever, personable, full of life. The fact we should all be in love with her was as inevitable as the phases of the moon.

'Your grandma's family, as I'm sure you know, was one of the wealthiest in town. They didn't have the Soutelos' power, but they certainly had more money. Her father, known as the Cuban, had amassed a fortune in Cuba.

The house of the Cuban! It was an amazing sight, with those towers none of us had ever seen. They pulled it down in the early seventies to build an ugly block of flats; a disaster, but that's another story there's no point going into right now.

'Your grandpa Pablo was also in love with Rosalía. He had the best chance of being successful; he was a Soutelo, heir to the manor, the only one who could match the Cuban's possessions. But who should Rosalía fall in love with except Rafael?

'I suppose there was nothing so unusual about this. Rafael was tall and handsome. He had a certain something which made him stand out wherever he went. It may have been the way he spoke, or his look, or just his natural intelligence. I've no idea how they met but, when I came back to Vilarelle that summer, the two of them were in love. They would see each other secretly. What else could they do? The Cuban was a right-wing fanatic and would kill his daughter if he saw her going out with a man like Rafael.

'It was my role to cover up for them. My family wasn't very rich, but it was prestigious; no one would find it strange for Rosalía to walk out with me, after all we were from the same social class. So frequently, in the afternoon, I'd head out with Rosalía and Susana, a friend of hers who was in on the secret. Once we had left the town, Rafael would join us. Susana and I would fall behind and let them walk ahead with each other, discussing their things. Sometimes – I don't suppose it matters if I say this – Rosalía would ask me to accompany her to Ishmael's workshop, where Rafael and Luís would be waiting for us. Luís and I would go upstairs to talk to Ishmael and they would stay on their own, it was the only time of intimacy they had together. They really were very in love, they planned to get married. But the war started and turned everything upside down.'

'What happened then? Because my grandmother ended up marrying Pablo.'

'Your grandpa Pablo, that's right. They married some years after the war ended. I suppose Rosalía got tired of waiting.'

'Waiting for what?'

'For news from Rafael. Since the outbreak of the war she hadn't heard from him.'

Sebastián then gave us an account of how the war turned a period of great enthusiasm into a time of death and bitterness. He told us about that summer in 1935, his long conversations with Luís and Rafael, which my grandfather would sometimes take part in, since he still had open ideas he would later abandon. He described the uprising in July 1936, which to his surprise reached Vilarelle as well, like a terrible wind. He explained how my grandfather, even though he later joined the soldiers, behaved very well towards the three of them. The Falangists – again the name of my grandmother's brother Héctor appeared – soon started hunting down anyone who'd expressed support for the Republic. My grandfather Pablo had managed to save the lives of Ishmael and Sebastián, who'd both spent years in prison but avoided being shot at the roadside. He also told us how Luís had escaped, taking to the mountains and reaching Republican territory. Everything he described was snippets of life, remnants which helped to complete the picture Hortensia had drawn a few days earlier.

'And Rafael? What happened to Rafael?' I asked, anxious that his name had not been mentioned.

'The Falangists really wanted to lay hands on Rafael but, when they went looking for him, they couldn't find him. They decided he must have gone, following Luís' footsteps, but they were wrong.' Sebastián stopped talking and stared at Miguel and me as if he knew the impact his next words would have. 'The fact is Rafael was hiding in the manor house, it was Pablo's idea, it was the perfect shelter, the only place the Falangists would never search. He must have been there for two or three weeks. Then he left. His plan was to set sail from Portugal for Buenos Aires.'

'But Gran said you never heard from him,' remarked Miguel.

'That's true, I don't know what can have happened, but we never heard from him again. He may not even have made it down to Portugal, it wasn't easy crossing the mountains. There were lots of unidentified bodies around that time.'

'How do you know all of this?' I asked.

'Rosalía told me. When I left prison, a few months after the war ended, I came back here, to my family. Rosalía paid me a visit, she wanted to know if any of the prisoners had news of Rafael. We carried on seeing each other, we were always good friends. It was then she explained to me what had happened, her despair at not hearing from Rafael, how grateful she was to Pablo for saving his life.'

'How come she ended up marrying Don Pablo?' asked Miguel. His words made me feel uncomfortable, I found it strange the way manor people were always referred to with such respect.

'At the end of the war Pablo became an important person. He was appointed mayor and later provincial governor... He acquired a lot of power, he could do whatever he liked.

'He married Rosalía in 1943. He'd carried on courting her, those years he tried to win her affection by whatever means. And Rosalía grew convinced that Rafael would never return. Pablo may have had his defects, but he wasn't a bad man; at least he didn't have blood on his hands, which was saying a lot back then. Later he became more corrupt, concerned only about the accumulation of wealth.'

Miguel asked more questions about Luís and Ishmael, with whom Sebastián had been in prison for some time. I suppose, like me, he was living the paradox of finding out important facts about his family from an outsider – if this man could be considered an outsider who'd been such good friends with people who lived only in our memory.

I remember we left Sebastián's home that evening in confusion. We knew lots more about certain things, it was true, but it was also increasingly obvious they had little to do with the stranger whose remains had turned up in the manor house. The ring may have been just a false clue which, as often happens, would end up leading nowhere.

12

July came to an end and the first days of August went by without anything unusual happening, if I can trust the notes in my diary. The renovations continued and, once work in the main building was complete, it was the turn of the enclosure wall. I had to leave the mirador on two or three mornings and go elsewhere, since the workmen's presence disturbed the silence and solitude I sought. It was strange to think that, had they fixed the wall a few weeks earlier, I would never have met Miguel. The guiding hand of chance, I now think, was on my side that time.

I carried on seeing Miguel three or four afternoons a week. Other days I couldn't because I was obliged to go with my cousin Ana to parties organized by the group of holidaymakers, which were a kind of torment for me. The girls were all like Ana or Teté, clones seemingly, who had no deeper concerns than boys or the dresses they were going to wear on each occasion. The boys, meanwhile, struck me as superficial and conceited, as if cut after the same pattern. I realized on the outside I looked like one of them; but on the inside, especially after all my conversations with Miguel, I felt I had nothing in common with these people who viewed the town's inhabitants like extras in a theme park.

For this reason my outings with Miguel became the

highlight of that summer. The confidence between us grew the more we knew each other, as did the physical attraction, even if I managed to disguise this in my diary with confessions laden with adolescent sentimentality. We still discussed the skeleton and the questions which had arisen as a result of our conversations with Hortensia and Sebastián, but there was no new information to help us escape the stalemate we were in.

My parents were as distant from me as ever. Daddy spent all his time in the manor, having begun his holidays at the start of August, and most days we had guests to lunch or dinner. They left me to my own devices and, apart from the dull parties I had to attend from time to time, as I said, and my obligatory presence at the sacred hour of lunch, I could do what I liked the rest of the day.

The only person I had a close relationship with in the manor was my uncle Carlos. Some evenings he'd come and visit me in my room, though mostly I would go to his. I always found him typing on his laptop, which was not such a common appliance as it is today. He'd brought one back from a trip to New York, which further increased the fascination I felt for my uncle. He never told me what he was typing, nor did I suspect he was writing the bitter account of his days, an unflattering reflection of his life which I now know also contained references to me.

I soon began to rely on my conversations with my uncle. I suppose, without necessarily meaning to, he was fulfilling the role of a father or the kind of older friend all of us seek in our youth, even if it's only to help us understand the complexity of life. Needless to say, I talked to him about Miguel and the deep friendship which had sprung up between us in a few weeks. But the day he showed the greatest interest was when I described the conversation we'd had with Sebastián, which, he explained, revealed aspects of his parents he'd never even imagined.

The tranquillity of those days was broken on the eighth of August. The pages I wrote in my diary that evening still bear the mark of the tears I must have shed as I attempted to explain what had happened, I was so upset and angry. I could tell it better now with the perspective of the years, even give it a touch of irony to make it less dramatic, but perhaps it's enough if I record here a few lines from the lengthy account in which I tried to express my pain:

What a horrible day! All I want to do is shut myself up in my room and cry till I've no tears left. I hate Daddy, I hate him more than ever, I shall never forgive him for what he did, I don't know how he can behave like that to me. He doesn't understand me, he doesn't listen to me, he never has. And I hate Mummy as well, she's a coward, she didn't say a word to defend me, even though she must have seen Daddy was being unfair. And in front of Ana and Alfredo, those two fools who could easily go back where they came from, I bet it was one of them who told him. Ana, for sure, who kept smiling innocently all the time, as if it had nothing to do with her. Or Alfredo, that pig, I've noticed him spying on me with those lecherous eyes of his, I should have forbidden him to come into my

*room after I caught him shuffling through the drawer
with my underwear in.*

*We were just having dinner when Daddy goes and
asks me in front of everyone if it was true that I was
going out with Miguel. He didn't call him that, he
probably doesn't even know his name, what he said
was 'that mechanic'. He knew things about him, he
knew he works in a garage, somebody must have
told him.*

*The question took me by surprise and I said yes.
I could have denied it, I should have been more
hypocritical. And then Daddy went wild, I'd never
seen him so annoyed. He banged his fist on the table,
the glasses all smashed on the floor, everyone was
frightened. And this was all because of me, all his
anger was because I was going out with Miguel.
'You're a Soutelo,' he said, 'you can't go gallivanting
about with a beggar! If I hear you've been seeing
him again, I'll shut you up in your room and you
won't come out for the rest of the summer. You've
been warned!'*

*Everyone was silent, looking at their feet, as he
carried on. Well, not everyone, Uncle Carlos was the
only one who raised his voice and made Daddy stop.
He's the only person in this family who understands
me, I don't know what I'd do if he wasn't here.*

If I close my eyes, I can still see the images of that evening:
Daddy's flushed face, Mummy's loyal silence, my cousins'
smug satisfaction, my own vain attempt to suppress my

tears in front of everyone. And then Carlos' defence as he got up from the table to accompany me to my room, where I could finally give vent to my tears and my frustration.

At around midnight there was a knock on the door. I didn't want to see anyone, especially not my mother or father, but I was relieved to hear Carlos' voice, he was the only person in the house I wanted to talk to. When he came in, I saw he was carrying a tray with some fruit and yoghurts.

'You can cry all you like, but you have to eat something,' he said once he'd got me to calm down and sit next to him. 'Don't worry, it's not the end of the world. Compared to the run-ins I had with my dad, this was nothing.'

As I couldn't stop sobbing, my uncle put his arm around me and held me tight while stroking my hair. After a little, he asked me:

'Do you love him?'

'Who?' I replied, though I knew perfectly well who he was referring to.

'Who do you think? This Miguel you've become such good friends with. I assumed he's the one you'd want to talk about.'

'I don't know, I don't know if I can say I love him. But he's the first boy I can be completely open with, when I'm with him I don't have to hide anything,' I answered, feeling a little comforted by Carlos' words. 'And I have to say I like him. I find him attractive, if that's what you mean.'

'I don't mean anything. I just want to know if you really want me to help you.'

'Help me do what?'

'Why, carry on seeing Miguel, of course!'

I raised my head and looked at him. My uncle had a mischievous expression on his face, he even seemed to be finding my predicament funny. It was then he explained his plan to me:

'You remember the story you told me about my mother and Rafael, that schoolteacher she was so in love with? Well, just as their friends helped them to see each other in secret, I'm going to help you. So stop crying and listen up.'

My uncle's plan was as perfect as it was simple. From that day on, Carlos would become my inseparable companion, at least in appearance. My parents would consider it normal, they knew how well we got on. And this would give them the guarantee that I'd ceased the inappropriate relationship they disliked so much. What they didn't know was that in fact Carlos would become my driver, the arranger of my meetings with Miguel.

We put the plan into action two days later. Carlos spoke to Miguel on the phone and gave him my message. That afternoon he drove me to the track leading to Charming Rock, where my friend would be waiting.

'Don't forget that officially we're visiting Monfero Monastery,' he said as I got out of the car. That was what he'd told my family at lunch, who seemed to find it only natural that Carlos should take me under his wing. 'It's four o'clock, we have to be back in the manor house at eight. So I want to see you here at seven thirty. Meanwhile I've other things to attend to.'

My uncle left and I ran down the track leading to

Charming Rock. There was Miguel, waiting for me. The first thing I did was embrace him, hug him tightly, I was eager to feel his body and taste his kisses again. Then, as we sat against the rock, I told him everything that had happened, from the argument with my father to Carlos' secret help.

'Deep down your father's not far wrong,' he said, having listened to me in silence. 'What am I, a garage mechanic, doing going out with a Soutelo girl? The world upside down, a commoner with a nobleman's daughter. I suppose Mum was right about that too.'

'What do you mean?'

'Mum also found it strange us being together. Though I know she only said this because she's afraid.'

'Afraid of what?'

'Afraid I'll get hurt when the summer's over and you leave. Afraid I might get ideas beyond my station.'

'And you? Are you afraid?' I asked, taken aback by his words. Miguel looked at me seriously and answered:

'You know I've always hated the holidaymakers, I can't help it. You come here for two months and show off the good life you lead, your cars, your clothes... I've always hated all of you, it's true, perhaps because you have what I'll never have: the whole day to read and go for walks, a university place assured, an easy future stretching out in front of you. Things will never be like that for me.'

I felt a lump in my throat and tears came into my eyes. Though he'd spoken calmly, Miguel's words were tinged with rage.

'Do you hate me too?' I asked him finally.

At that point his look changed. He pulled me towards him and ever so gently stroked my face.

'How could I hate you? I barely know you and you're already the best friend I ever had. I can't bear to think I'll have to leave you one day, it hurts me terribly. And besides, you're not like them. If you were, you wouldn't be here now.'

I remember we talked for a lot longer and swore eternal friendship. I remember we kissed again and again, happy to be there, in this secret place where we felt isolated from the world. And I remember the time passed quickly, as it usually does when you're happy.

At seven thirty we climbed the path back to the road. My uncle soon appeared. When he stopped the car, I introduced him to Miguel. My friend was a little embarrassed at first, but Carlos' warm manner soon won him over.

'Is everything OK?' my uncle asked when we were in the car and had left Miguel, who was going to cycle back to town.

'Wonderful, uncle!' I didn't need to say anything, I suppose the expression on my face was proof enough. 'I owe you one, you know.'

'Well, I expect you in my room after dinner. I've lots to tell you.'

'Why's that?' I asked, suddenly intrigued.

'I didn't go to Monfero Monastery today either, as you can imagine. In fact I went to Betanzos, where the coroner who examined the skeleton lives. You'll be amazed by what she had to say.'

13

During dinner my uncle gave a very convincing account of our visit to Monfero, lingering over details which surprised even me, they sounded so credible. He ended up lamenting the state of disrepair the monastery had fallen into, various parts having collapsed which were now overgrown with brambles. Later, when my parents settled down in the sitting room next to the porch to drink their coffee, I went up to Carlos' room as quickly as possible. My uncle had always been a bit of an actor and that evening, from his tone of voice, I'd noticed he had something important to tell me.

He started by explaining he'd had another conversation with my father a few days before, since he wanted to know how the investigations into the case were going. Unlike Miguel and me, who were primarily interested in finding out the identity of the corpse, my uncle was far more drawn to another question: who wielded the pistol which fired two bullets and caused that person's death?

As on other occasions, my father had tried to avoid giving straight answers. These were stories which belonged to the past, the case had already prescribed, the judge had expressed his willingness to file the documents and to stop pestering them. And the only official report he had was the draft prepared by the coroner on the day the body was removed. He expected to receive a copy of all the documents once proceedings had drawn to a close.

'I know your father very well, I lived with him for many years, so I soon realized he was lying. Or hiding something, to be exact. He unwittingly confirmed this to me when he referred to an official report, as I'll explain. I then understood that, if I wanted to know more, I'd have to act on my own.'

'I can't see why Daddy would want to hide something,' I remarked. 'What difference does it make?'

'I have a few answers to that question, but I'm still not sure, so I prefer to leave it for now,' replied Carlos.

'But you've found out something new, haven't you?'

'I got lucky. I couldn't do anything with the judge, he's under your father's influence and would soon tell him of my interest.' Carlos came closer and added, 'But life's full of surprises. The coroner, Isabel Riveiro, is an old friend of mine. She was one of the best friends I had in Santiago, the only person in the party who knew about my homosexuality.'

'The party? What party?' I interrupted him.

'I was a member of the Galician Socialist Party back then, I'll tell you about it some other day. The fact is Isabel and I shared not just political views, but lots of other interests. There was no film club or exhibition we hadn't been to, lots of our friends thought there was something going on between us. We never bothered to correct their mistake, in fact we did what we could to encourage it. Later, when I moved to Barcelona, I lost track of her. And now I find she's married, living in Betanzos, and she's the coroner on this case. Life's funny little coincidences!'

'So you spoke to her,' I ventured.

'For the second time today, the first time was last week. Then she gave me a copy of her final report, but I asked her to get me a copy of the other official documents, which she gave me today.'

I was taken aback. If these documents existed, my father must also have a copy. In which case, why was he hiding them? I decided to wait for my uncle to reveal what else he knew. I was in for further surprises.

'I also agreed to take her my father's pistol today, but I couldn't, because I couldn't find it.'

'Grandpa had a pistol?' I was amazed.

'He did, yes. I'll tell you about it in a bit, because I'm going to need your help. But first let me explain things to you in order.'

My uncle picked up a folder which was on the table and opened it. He pulled out several sheets of paper and, holding them, continued:

'This is a copy of all the official documents: the removal of the body, the coroner's two reports and the statements the judge took from whoever he thought was necessary, including your father.' Carlos stared at me for a moment and added, 'I don't have to tell you that all this is confidential, I would hate to get Isabel in trouble. You can't tell Miguel, this has to stay between me and you. Family secrets, like in novels.'

'I'm like the grave, uncle,' I replied, though inside I was far from sure I'd be able to keep this from Miguel. 'What do the documents say?'

'About the removal of the body I think you know everything, you were there after all. Though there may be something you missed, perhaps because you were paying too much attention to that ring. There were four coins from the time of the Republic in among the carpet remains. So now we know for certain that the murder was committed after 1931, and before 1937, which is when Franco started to circulate his own coinage. However, there were no personal documents. Either they rotted or someone emptied his pockets before walling up the body.'

'And doesn't the coroner give an exact date?'

'The report is very detailed, even unpleasant, but that's all there is. Isabel explained she couldn't be more precise about the date. Though the coins narrow it down somewhat.

'She does give more information about other aspects. A man between twenty and thirty years of age, tall, about five foot ten, no distinguishing features worth mentioning. Murdered obviously, either of the bullets could have caused his death. One went in through the back of his right temple, he must have been shot from behind. The other may have pierced his heart, there are signs of impact on two of the ribs.'

Carlos paused. It was clear he hadn't finished. In the meantime I tried to tie in all that information with what I already knew.

'What you say could fit what we know about Rafael, the schoolteacher,' I suggested. 'Then there's the ring I found with the letter "R". Do you think it's him?'

'I'm not sure, there's nothing really to allow us to

make that affirmation,' replied Carlos. 'Why him and not somebody else? To know for certain, we'd have to carry out a DNA test.'

I'd never heard of this test, back then it was still rare and expensive, it would be years before it was as common as it is today. My uncle explained what it was about and then added:

'To do it, we'd have to find a relative of this Rafael. And we don't know anything about him, except what those two people told you. Anyway, as I already said, I'm more interested in finding out who wielded the murder weapon.'

'How do you know it was a pistol?'

'The first time I saw Isabel, she gave me the results of the bullet analysis. She had a report from the ballistics department in Coruña. The bullets were fired by a Browning 25-calibre automatic pistol. As you probably know from watching films, you can tell the exact gun which fired the bullets from the marks it leaves on the cartridge.'

'But there must be lots of those guns.'

'It was a common model back then, that's true. What you don't know is that my father had one of them. He used to show it to us when we were children, much to my mother's anger, she couldn't bear weapons. I remember we were all fascinated. It was small and light, a dark metallic grey colour with mother-of-pearl grips. I can close my eyes and see it.'

'Do you think that was the gun which fired the bullets?'

'I do. Now perhaps you understand why I'm so keen to find out who wielded the weapon.'

'Then all you have to do is give the coroner the pistol so she can have it analysed.'

'That's what I thought,' my uncle replied. 'Daddy's gun was always in the glass cabinet in his office, together with the medals and decorations he received. But there's no weapon there now. I asked your father about it and he said he hadn't seen it in years, perhaps Mummy got rid of it after Daddy died. But that's a lie, I saw it there long after that. Besides, I know Víctor too well, as I told you, I can tell when he's lying.'

'Why would he lie? I'm not sure I know where you're heading.'

'Nor am I, though I have my theories. For example, I'm convinced it was your father who removed that pistol. Can you believe in his statement he told the judge there had never been small arms in the manor house, only hunting rifles? Why lie like that?'

'Supposing you're right, where's the pistol now?' I asked.

'I don't know, but I can guess. And I need you to check it for me.'

'Me? What can I do?'

'The following. I think it must be in your parents' bedroom. I searched all the other rooms in the manor house yesterday and today, I even looked behind the books in the library, but to no avail.'

I was amazed by what my uncle was telling me, it was as if a secret history were unfolding in front of me without my knowledge. So Carlos had been investigating the case for several days? Well, he must be a highly skilful detective, because no one had noticed.

'I can't go in their bedroom. If somebody found me there, I'd have no excuse,' he added. 'But you can, all you have to say is you've gone to get something of your mother's.'

I couldn't deny Carlos anything, though I wasn't entirely sure about his intentions. So it was that I was drawn into an intrigue which, were I to be discovered, could seriously damage the already strained relationship I had with my father.

14

The first chance I had to enter my parents' bedroom without anyone seeing me came one afternoon, two days after the conversation with Carlos. Mummy and Daddy had gone to a party organized by some friends in Pontedeume and wouldn't be back until well after midnight. The twins and Alfredo had accompanied my uncle to Coruña for the premiere of the latest Indiana Jones film. And my cousin Ana was going out with her new boyfriend, having finally got the attention of the boy she'd been pursuing since the start of the summer. Celsa and Brais wouldn't leave the manor but, since there was little to do, they'd be downstairs, in the kitchen, watching television.

The time was right, I had to make a decision. I entered my parents' room in a state of panic. Once inside, I observed the different pieces of furniture and came up with a plan to search them in order. First of all, I went through the drawers in the bedside tables, and then in the desk next to the gallery. There were lots of things there, obviously, and some of them aroused my curiosity, but they weren't what I was looking for. I then searched inside the chest of drawers and the wardrobe. Shoes, bags, all sorts of clothes... There was nothing in there which wasn't predictable.

When I attempted to examine the cabinet next to the chest of drawers, I found the door was locked. I'd seen various keys when I searched the bedside tables, so I went and got them and tried them all, in the hope that one might fit. But none of them did.

I left the room soon afterwards, taking care to erase any traces of my presence, my hands as empty as when I'd gone in. Though I did have more information. The cabinet was now my main goal, there wasn't much sense in it being the only piece of furniture which was locked. If Carlos was correct in his suspicions, the key must be with my father, this was the only logical conclusion. He always carried a large key ring in his pocket, so I guessed that's where the key would be.

The whole of the next day, I didn't let my father out of my sight, waiting for an opportunity to get hold of the key ring. The opportunity came in the afternoon when, after lunch, my father went for a siesta in one of the hammocks in the garden. It was hot, he was wearing only his shorts and a vest. As soon as I felt no one was watching me, I went upstairs and, instead of going to my bedroom, entered my parents' room. Just as I'd expected, the key ring was on his bedside table, next to his wallet and sunglasses.

I took the keys and hurried over to the cabinet. Trying to control my nerves, I checked to see if one of them would fit, and I was lucky. The third key I introduced into the lock opened the door easily. Aware that I'd have a problem explaining my presence there if I was caught, I quickly scoured the contents of the different drawers. Most of them contained papers and folders full of official documents. But in the bottom drawer, concealed by four smaller folders, I finally found what I was looking for. There was the pistol, in a brown leather holster worn away by the passing of time. The pistol with the mother-of-pearls grips my uncle had described, and the name Browning engraved on the dark metal of the barrel.

As I held it in my hands, I was overcome by doubts. What was I to do? The logical thing would have been to take it and to give it to Carlos, so through the coroner he could make the tests he wanted. If my uncle was right, the case could take a new direction, though in practice it might be a false move, since before the law it proved nothing new. The temptation to leave it there, however, was very strong, I didn't even want to consider what would happen if Daddy went looking for it and found it missing.

I was having these doubts when I heard my mother's voice in the sitting room next to the porch. She was telling my father that they'd have to get ready soon if they didn't want to be late for some appointment. This meant they'd be coming up to the bedroom and would catch me inside, and then I'd find it impossible to provide a convincing excuse.

I suppose it was the instinct which awakens inside us when we're in danger which made me put the pistol back in the drawer, lock the cabinet and place the keys on the bedside table. And then, as I heard my parents climb the stairs, I could only think to hide under the bed and to wait there, lying still and holding my breath.

And there I remained, on the floor, without moving a muscle, sweat dripping from my pores, fearing all the time that the drum beats of my heart would give me away. My parents chatted to each other, oblivious to my discomfort. It was a normal, routine conversation, but even so I felt like an intruder, since they mentioned intimacies it wasn't right for me to hear. From where I was, I could see their feet moving about the room, so close I could have touched them. At one point Mummy sat down on the bed to put on the shoes she'd chosen, and then I thought I was bound to be discovered.

But luckily nothing happened. My parents finished getting ready and left the room. I allowed a few more minutes to pass, until I heard the front door close and the sound of the car pulling away. I then came out of my hiding-place and left, fear still coursing through my veins. I soon made it to my room. I was safe at last, though I hadn't managed to take the gun.

'Don't worry about it,' Carlos tried to cheer me up that evening, when I told him about my discovery. 'Now we know where the pistol is and we have confirmation your father hid it, even if we don't know the reasons. That's quite something. I can now be sure it fired the bullets. Otherwise why would your father want to hide it? Why keep it from his own brother?'

'I suppose so, but it doesn't seem much. And you have to admit it doesn't tell us anything about the victim,' I replied, mentioning what I was most interested in. 'If only we knew something else about that Rafael! If we could find a relative of his who could confirm whether he left for Argentina or not. All we know is he was in the town, we don't even have a clue where he came from.'

Despite my words, the truth is I was slowly beginning to realize the implications of my find. My grandfather's pistol had been used to kill a man who'd then been walled up, even if we didn't know who'd been holding the gun. And my father clearly didn't want these facts to be revealed, since it seemed obvious he was the one who'd hidden it. Why would my father, a notary of some repute, bother to do this? Did he know something Carlos and I didn't? I felt the calm waters my family appeared to move in were serene only on the surface, and sensed that deep down there reigned darkness and turbulence.

15

The following day, still puzzled by my discovery of the previous afternoon, I decided to visit my grandmother Rosalía's room. The motive to do so came from the words Sebastián had spoken as soon as he saw me: 'Her face is in yours, you're very similar'. Hortensia had said the same thing when we met. Were my grandmother and I really so alike?

There were lots of photos of Rosalía in the manor house, but they were photographs taken after she got married. Normally she appeared with one of her children or on one of the many trips she'd gone on with my grandfather. And they all showed a beautiful, elegant woman, even when she was old. There were also several albums in the drawers of the sideboard in the sitting room, with various photos, some of which were the same as those in the rest of the house. All these images recorded the passing of the years, you could write a biography of my grandmother and her family from them. But this biography began from the date of her marriage, as if her life had started in the year 1943. There wasn't a single photo of my grandmother when she was young, nothing I could use to compare myself to the girl Hortensia and Sebastián had known. And yet they had to exist. They must be somewhere, possibly in her bedroom.

Here I could go about my investigations without fear of being discovered. My grandmother's room had remained closed since the day she'd died, nothing had been touched in the intervening period. The maids only went in two or three times a week to air it and to take the dust. And they'd aired it the day before, I'd made sure of that, so there was no danger of someone interrupting my visit.

It was a large room, though not as big as others in the manor house. When I went in, the room was in shade, lit by a few rays of light which filtered through the cracks in the shutters. I opened wide two windows and the sunlight poured in, flooding the whole room and allowing me a clear view of what until then had been a succession of shadows.

There was the furniture I remembered so well, which had always seemed enormous to me as a child. It was all made of chestnut wood, varnished a dark colour made more pronounced by the passing of time, a colour which seemed to confirm the wood's solid appearance. There was the bed, with the carved headboard which drew my attention, and the matching night tables. The impressive three-door wardrobe, where I'd often hidden during our childhood games, occupying almost a whole wall. The large, spacious chest of drawers, with vegetable motifs decorating the front, and the mirror on top, its quicksilver surface slightly corroded. The picture of the Sacred Heart which, as my mother used to say while laughing, terrified me so much when I was little. The easy chairs upholstered in green velvet, like the armchair in front of the desk. And me there, in the middle, gazing at this furniture I'd known as a girl. I saw it differently now, like the remains of a period which had frozen in time the day Grandma Rosalía died. And, although I was now bigger, I quickly looked away from the picture over the bed, which still managed to arouse my childish fears.

I was primarily interested in photos, but I lingered over the other objects I came across as I opened doors and drawers. The wardrobe full of clothes which would one day have to be thrown out: blouses, skirts, suits, coats, most of them grey or other dark colours. The chest of drawers stuffed with sweaters, shirts and underwear. The only surprise was in the bottom drawer, where I found the album of stamps Grandma had collected during a period of her life, an album I'd been fascinated in due to the colour and variety of stamps which transported me to distant, exotic countries.

If there were photographs, and there had to be, it was clear they must be in one of the night tables or the desk. In the drawers in the night tables, all I found was a rosary, a missal, various prayer books and a veritable arsenal of medicines. There were also some papers, most of them worthless documents and receipts, as I was quickly able to confirm.

I then headed for the desk and sat in the green velvet armchair in front of it. The desk was an astonishing artefact, bigger than most furniture of this kind, since it was well over sixty inches wide. As a girl playing hide-and-seek with my cousin, I'd sometimes hidden under the rolling screen which covered the whole of the desktop surface. A secret refuge I'd loved, though I'd always been afraid of not being able to open it again.

I rolled back the screen, revealing the desktop surface. Just as I remembered, it was divided into lots of small drawers and narrow compartments of varying length. What was in them was predictable: writing paper, envelopes of different sizes, all yellowed by the years, pens and biros, a collection of tiny ceramic and glass figures of animals, religious medallions, various stamps... but no photographs.

I turned my attention to the three drawers at the front, located under the desk. The middle one, which was the widest, was bulging with letters. I soon discovered they were mostly years old, from my father, uncle and aunt. There were also some from other relatives and people I'd never heard of. There they were, silent witnesses of a period I didn't belong to, since the postmarks were all from before I was born.

I found the photographs in the right drawer, in various cardboard boxes, each a different colour as if each box had its own theme. Many were photos of her grandchildren, some of me when I was a girl. There were also some of family get-togethers, and others of her with Grandpa and the children, some of which I'd already seen in the albums in the sitting room. But there still weren't any photos showing my grandmother as a girl or teenager. I was well aware at that time photography was a minority hobby, available only to the small sector of society which could afford such a luxury; but I was surprised that my grandmother's family, which had come from Cuba and been so rich, hadn't left a photographic record of their years of splendour.

When I opened the left drawer, I realized my search was over. There, in a small album with faded red covers, were the photographs which showed Grandma Rosalía's life before she was married. Family photographs, with what must have been her parents and brothers, photographs with groups of girlfriends, and photographs on her own, most of them studio portraits. And yes, it moved me to see them, as if I'd suddenly been taken back in time, given other clothes and another hairstyle, and placed in front of the camera's probing eye.

It was like looking in the mirror, except that what was reflected back was somebody else's life. The eyes were mine, as were the mouth and oval face. The expression may have been different, but Sebastián was right. Genetic chance had turned me into an almost exact physical copy of my grandmother. It was strange to recognize myself in these photographs from the past, since we tend to think we're unique and unrepeatable. Of course we are, but not in our physical appearance: there are always relatives, sometimes distant, who live on in us through our features, as if handing down an inheritance we have no right to renounce.

I decided to keep some of these photos, I was sure nobody would miss them. I took out the drawer and placed it on the desk in order to choose them more easily. It was then I noticed the drawer was much shorter than it should have been, given the desk's depth. Intrigued, I took out the right drawer as well in order to compare them. There was no doubt: the left drawer was about eight inches shorter than the other one. How could a desk of such quality contain such a defect?

I squatted down and peered into the two hollows. It was obvious the one on the left was not so deep. Unclear why this should be so, I felt inside and realized there was a small depression in the upper surface, a place which seemed made for you to put your fingertips. When I pressed on the surface, I heard a click and the piece at the end moved. I pulled it towards me and discovered to my amazement there was something there, a second, smaller drawer designed to remain hidden behind the first. A very clever way to keep something secret.

This new drawer was almost entirely filled by a wooden box. Overcome by curiosity, I opened it. Inside were two folded pieces of paper, the edges so marked they threatened to break irremediably. Beneath these were three photos and a silver necklace, darkened by time. I wouldn't have paid it much attention had it not been for an oval plaque hanging from the chain with an ornate letter engraved on it. The same letter 'R' as on the ring I kept in my bedside table. In one of the corners of the box, there was also a small glass jar with a transparent liquid.

I unfolded the pages, taking care not to break them. I only had to read the first and last lines to realize I was holding two letters: 'My darling Rosalía', 'Rafael'. A shiver ran down my spine. What was it chance – chance again – had placed in my hands?

Without thinking about it, I replaced the drawers and made sure everything was as I'd found it. I closed the windows and, having checked to see the corridor was empty, left the room with that surprising wooden box in my hands. Minutes later, I was in my bedroom, ready to examine these pieces of life which had come to me from the depths of time.

16

The first thing I did was examine the photos. One of them was a full-length portrait of a young man in a suit and tie. The man was tall and athletic-looking, with dark, curly hair; he had an attractive face, in which the most noticeable feature was his deep, happy eyes. I knew this man had to be Rafael when I turned over the portrait, since on the back was a dedication in the same handwriting I'd just seen in the letters: 'To Rosalía, forever in my heart'. I didn't even need the letters to know this, such a dedication could only be from the great love of her youth.

The second photo was a group portrait, showing Rafael next to some other young men in a place I soon recognized, since behind them you could see the obelisk at the start of Cantóns Avenue in Coruña. The third photo was a full-length portrait of Rafael and Rosalía together. I couldn't tell then where it had been taken, nor can I now, when I look at it again. It's clear they're in the country, since the ground is covered with grass and there's a birch tree in the centre of the picture. My grandmother is in front of the tree, covering it slightly, while Rafael, a step back, leans his right shoulder against the trunk. It must have been autumn because the trees in the background still have some of their leaves. Rafael is wearing a long coat, which is unbuttoned, my grandmother a light-coloured skirt suit, with a thin striped jersey underneath, which is possibly white and navy blue. She's adopted a coquettish pose, her right leg slightly bent, her hand in one of the jacket pockets. Rafael, holding a cigarette, looks more spontaneous, as if he were unaware of the eye which would immortalize them. The two of them are looking at the camera and smiling: Rosalía openly, her eyes seem to be giving off sparks of happiness; Rafael less obviously, there's more of a glint in his eyes than in the form of his mouth.

The reason I can describe it so accurately is that this photograph occupies a privileged place in my house, not a day goes by that I don't exchange glances with the two of them. Who took the photo? Who can have captured this moment of happiness between two lovers? I don't know, but I do know I'd like someone, one day, to take a similar photo of me, to immortalize me in one of those rare moments of happiness life gives us.

Having carefully examined the photos, I prepared to read the letters. I have them in front of me as I write these lines, I kept them all these years together with the other things in that box. It was Carlos who insisted I keep them, he was content with photocopies. They're even more worn now than when I first read them, the ink has continued fading, but I can still make out the small handwriting, the rounded, perfect form of the letters.

My darling Rosalía,

The first thing I must ask is for you to burn this letter when you've read it, don't let anyone see, it shouldn't fall into the hands of someone else, especially someone from your family. I don't suppose you know what Héctor's been up to, better that way, you can't share the same blood I had to overcome Pablo's resistance, he thinks it a great risk my writing to you, it could put us both in grave danger if someone knew where I was. Writing to you, I risk my life and Pablo risks his security, since there are those who would consider the help he is giving me an act of betrayal.

I've been in the attic of the manor house since the twenty-sixth. It was that night Pablo came to warn me I was on the list of targets to be eliminated in Vilarelle. I'm a teacher, I defend the Republican government, I belong to the Galicianist Party, I'm a member of the cultural association. These are the charges against me. It doesn't make sense, it's like a nightmare, but it isn't, the darkest predictions have ended up coming true.

I don't wish to sadden you, this letter is for you to know that I'm well. I spend the day on my own, the hours here last an eternity. I try not to make any noise, even the servants don't know about me. Pablo comes at night and we both go down to a small room under the stairs. He brings me food for the next day, and a few books, and tells me what's happening outside.

I learned from him that Ishmael and Sebastián were arrested and are in Betanzos Prison. I asked him about the other members of the party: Edelmiro, Xosé, Amancio, Antón... He remained silent when I asked, so everything points to their being dead.

I don't know anything about Luís, though Pablo assures me he wasn't taken prisoner or killed. Perhaps he managed to escape, which was his idea. The day before I went into hiding, I spoke to him and he said there were people in Betanzos who planned to leave for Asturias; they calculated it would take them three or four days, walking by night and hiding during the day. He wanted to join the Republican army and fight against Franco's soldiers. I hope he managed to do so. Luís doesn't deserve to die so young, none of us does.

Last night Pablo suggested I should stay hidden in the manor house until things calm down locally, you know better than me how bad things are. But this uprising can't last long, the rule of law has to prevail. Perhaps in a few weeks we can be together again and start that new life we both want.

I'm running out of space, this is the only paper I have. I just want you to know, darling Rosalía, I think about you every minute, the memory of you is the only thing which enables me to resist the anxiety gnawing inside me. I don't lose hope, I never will so long as you love me.

I love you, I love you as I never thought it possible to love another.

Rafael

This was the first letter. Whenever I read it, I can easily imagine the anxiety felt by this man I never met, an anxiety I suppose my grandmother shared when she received it. Only a few months ago, I read some verses by a Polish poet, Wisława Szymborska, which always come to my mind when I look at Rafael's letters: 'We read the letters of the dead like helpless gods, / but gods, nonetheless, since we know the dates that follow'. Yes, we know what Rafael and Rosalía never knew or could have imagined. We know that tragedy was waiting around the corner and they would never share the life they dreamed of. We know about the ferociousness of the war, the murdering of the noblest members of that generation, the terrible postwar period when people like my grandfather got so rich. Money born of blood, violence, fear. And then my father goes and calls me a rebel! A rebel, yes; when you know how things were, you have no other path open to you than that of your conscience. This was something else Carlos taught me.

But I must go back to my story, the best way I have to settle scores with the past. There was, as I said, a second letter, written eight days later:

August 10th

My darling Rosalía,
I shall never be able to thank Pablo enough for
what he's doing for me. You and I, when we're safe
and together again, owe him a debt of gratitude,
notwithstanding the huge political differences between

us. The soldiers see in him the natural leader for this region, they think he should be at the front of the local junta they're going to form. Pablo agrees and is going to accept, he told me this morning.

Yes, this morning, these days I've been staying in a room next to his, since there's no danger of being found out. His parents have left to spend some time in Santiago and he's forbidden the servants to come upstairs.

Pablo thinks the next days are ideal for me to make my escape. We've been working out the safest route: from here across the border to Portugal and down to Porto. He's going to write me a letter of recommendation for a friend he has there. From Porto I'll be able to board a ship for Buenos Aires, as others are doing. And in Buenos Aires I'll wait for this absurd war to be over. As soon as I can, I'll send you news, for you to know everything's worked out well, as I so eagerly wish.

My plan is to leave on the fourteenth. That night there's a new moon, the perfect time to start my journey. Trust me. And please don't disclose the role Pablo's played, we'd get him into a lot of trouble. These days he's shown me how friendship for him comes above ideas. Something valuable in times like these. I'll never forget it.

From today I shall start counting the days until I see you, my darling. Your love will always be at my side, accompanying me.

Rafael

My first impulse on finishing these letters was to go and find my uncle Carlos. But I would have to wait, since he'd taken the boys out for the day. I spent the intervening hours rereading the letters in a state of impatience. It was after nine when they returned. We then had to have dinner and sit around afterwards as on any normal day. It was close to midnight when he finally retired to his bedroom. I quickly followed him upstairs and found him at the computer, typing that text he never let me see, the text I would only get to read after his death. I asked him to come with me to my room and, seeing the expression on my face, he immediately got up and turned off the computer.

Once we were in my room, I showed him the objects I'd found in the box. He was a lot more impressed than I'd expected. He read both letters several times, as if he wished to learn them by heart. And, as I'd done, he gazed at the necklace and photos for ages, I suppose he was surprised to have the stories we'd heard over the previous weeks confirmed.

'Grandma kept her secrets to herself,' I remarked when Carlos finally put the photos on the table. 'Did you never suspect anything?'

'How could I? I'm as amazed as you are,' my uncle answered. 'But, to tell the truth, I'm even more surprised about my father. I'm glad to know he was capable of doing something good and altruistic at some point in his life.'

'Now we know Hortensia and Sebastián's stories were true,' I added. 'And that the skeleton we found could belong to anyone, but not to Rafael.'

Carlos was about to reply, but fell silent when he noticed the glass jar inside the box.

'What's this?'

'I've no idea. It was in the box as well,' I answered. 'It looks like medicine.'

'It does, yes, but there's no label.'

My uncle opened the jar and smelled the contents. He then turned it upside down with a finger on the opening and, placing the jar on the table, licked the tip of his finger several times. He didn't talk, but a shadow swept across his face.

'If you don't mind, I'm going to take this jar. I'd like to know what's inside.' He then pointed to the box and added, 'You should keep the rest hidden away and not tell anyone. For now it's best if this remains just between the two of us.'

'But I'll have to tell Miguel,' I objected. 'He's been involved since the beginning, we can trust him.'

'Tell him if you want, I'm sure he won't say anything. It's your parents I meant.'

Carlos stood up and walked towards the door. He was about to open it when he stopped and turned around.

'Talking of Miguel, did you know tomorrow night's the meteor shower? There'll be some tonight as well, the famous night of St Lawrence, but the best time to see them is tomorrow, the eleventh. And it seems the sky will be clear. You don't want to miss such an opportunity.'

I'd heard of the 'tears of St Lawrence', a shower of shooting stars visible in the sky in August. The year we spent the summer in Pontedeume, I'd gone out to see them with my uncle and my mother. We'd climbed up to the chapel and followed a path to a natural viewpoint. There was no light at all, just a tiny glow from the sky covering us like a protective blanket. It had been quite an adventure and I'd found watching stars shoot across the dark sky a fascinating spectacle. But I hadn't realized it was that date already; when you're on holiday, you end up losing all track of time.

'What does the meteor shower have to do with Miguel?'

'Come, Clara, don't be so ingenuous. I thought you'd like to see them together. This is an experience which has to be shared, otherwise it loses all its charm,' my uncle had adopted a suggestive look 'I'm going to invite you to come and see them with me tomorrow after dinner, so you know what you have to do.'

And with that he opened the door and walked out, leaving me feeling flushed at the wonderful opportunity he'd just offered me.

17

At lunch the following day, my uncle made a remark about the meteor shower that night and invited me to go and view them with him, as if the idea had just occurred to him. Nobody was surprised; at performances like this, Carlos was an expert. To start with, the twins and Alfredo wanted to come along and for a few minutes I was afraid our plans would be spoiled. I'd already called Miguel at home and arranged to pick him up between ten thirty and eleven at the chapel where we used to meet. But I was in luck and the boys soon changed their mind. They preferred to attend a dinner-dance the holidaymakers organized every Saturday at the casino club. As for my cousin Ana, there was no problem: she wasn't interested in stars or anything else which would prevent her from dancing the night away with her new conquest.

Everything went as we'd expected. We left the manor in my uncle's car a little before eleven. We picked up Miguel, who'd been waiting for a while, and then took the road to Betanzos. I still thought we'd head for a local mirador and view the stars the three of us. It was enough for me to spend a few hours with Miguel, even if it was in the company of Carlos. But I was taken aback when, on reaching the track leading down to the river, my uncle stopped the car and said:

'I'll pick you up in the same place at one o'clock. That

should be time enough for you to see all the stars you want.'

Then, when he realized Miguel had nothing with him, he turned to me staring back from the passenger seat in amazement and added:

'Fetch a sleeping bag there is in the boot. It may be August, but the grass will be cold from the night dew, especially next to the river. Take the torch as well, you may need it.'

I got out of the car and fetched the things my uncle had suggested. Miguel, who'd already got out, was waiting by the door in silence; I think, like me, he hadn't got over his surprise. My uncle drove away and left us there, watching the tail lights fade into the distance.

We both went down the track we knew so well. It was a clear night, despite the absence of the moon, so we didn't need the torch. When we reached Charming Rock, we opened the sleeping bag and placed it so that we could lean against the rock and gaze into the sky's vastness above the road, since it was in the east where most of the stars would be visible.

If being there was like being on a desert island, the feeling of solitude was intensified at night, as if the darkness joined forces with us to create an even more remote and intimate setting. There was the murmur of the water and the rustling of the treetops swaying in the wind. From time to time we heard a frog croak and crickets sing, and the dull, constant whirring of grasshoppers all over the meadow.

If a shooting star crossed the sky during that first part of the night, we didn't see it. I feel tenderness as I read the words I wrote a few hours later in my diary, shamelessly romantic, but they convey the passion of that night. The sentences are full of the kind of metaphors you can only use when you're sixteen, with the whole of your life in front of you. Ridiculous perhaps, but still evocative. Now, as I return to them again, I feel the burning sensations I experienced back then. Miguel's hands travelling over my body, mine caressing his, the sweet, sweet kisses, deep and unforgettable as only those we give our first love can be. And the words, overused perhaps, but to us it was as if they were being spoken for the first time. The discovery of so many inner emotions, since while up above the stars streaked momentarily across the sky, another shower of stars burst from deep inside me, filling my body with a warm glow. I can't help feeling a stab of nostalgia now, when I realize I'll never have that experience again, since there's only one first time in life.

I remember, however, that there was still time for shooting stars and we gazed at the sky for more than an hour, in a happy embrace, following the luminous lines which shot across the sky, always in surprising directions. Dozens of shooting stars which went with our desires, as if that night sky were an inexhaustible Aladdin's lamp showering us with favours.

It was after these moments of happiness that I told Miguel about the letters and photos I'd discovered. We tried to piece together the love story my grandmother and that unknown Rafael had experienced so many years previously. Their secret meetings, which reminded us of ours; the pain of separation, the despair the letters transmitted. And the disappointment she must have felt when the months went by without any news from her beloved.

A little before one, we realized our happy interlude was over. We picked up the sleeping bag and climbed the track to the road, a journey I was now familiar with. Holding hands, and joyful as you can only be when love makes you feel so alive that nothing else matters. We didn't care about anything other than our relationship, even if we sensed it was impossible. But at times like that you don't think about it, or at least I didn't, judging by the passionate notes in my diary.

My uncle arrived at the prearranged hour. He never said whether he'd gone to see the stars somewhere or simply whiled away the hours until our meeting. We got in the car and journeyed back in silence, answering Carlos' questions with monosyllables. Shortly before arriving, Miguel suddenly put his hand to his head and remarked:

'I almost forgot! Carme, Sebastián's niece, rang. Now he's the one who wants to see us. She asked if we could go on Monday afternoon, around five. Can you?'

I said I could, I was sure Carlos and I could come up with a suitable excuse. We soon reached the place where we'd picked up Miguel, who took his leave of me with the briefest of kisses. I watched him through the back window, happy and sorrowful at the same time, as he stood in the middle of the road, his eyes on the car returning to the manor house.

Later, in my room, I couldn't get to sleep for ages. I kept going over the hours we'd spent by the river, lying under that sky criss-crossed by shooting stars. Wonderful hours, perhaps the only ones I will remember when my life is over and all I hold is the memory of moments of happiness.

18

O n Monday, shortly before the prearranged time, I took my bike and left the manor with the excuse that I had to buy some felt-tip pens in town. When I reached the square, Miguel was waiting for me in front of Sebastián's house. He greeted me with a quick kiss on the cheek and helped me put the bike in the garden. Carme had already seen us because she opened the door before we could ring the bell.

This time we knew the way, so we headed straight for the gallery. There was Sebastián, in his armchair, as if he hadn't moved since our last visit. We greeted him and sat down in the chairs we'd occupied before.

'The more I see you, the more you remind me of Rosalía,' he said, staring at me with an intensity which made me go red. It was the second time I'd heard this from him, but now I had in my mind the image of the photos I'd discovered. 'Though I think perhaps you're more beautiful,' he added.

Carme brought a tray with coffee and biscuits, as on the other day, but today she didn't leave. She took a chair and sat down next to us, barely intervening the whole time we were there.

'I sent for you because our last conversation left me feeling unsettled. I am constantly haunted by memories, I can't stop thinking about all those years.'

'You'll have to excuse us, Sebastián,' Miguel apologized. 'That wasn't our intention.'

'I know, I know. It's sometimes painful to remember, but I don't think it's bad; it was my life, after all. But I didn't invite you to tell you that.' Sebastián's expression changed and, looking at me, he added, 'All those questions the other day, they wouldn't have something to do with that skeleton I understand turned up in the manor house, would they?'

'To a certain extent, yes,' I replied. 'The corpse could have been there since the war years, at least that's what I've been told.'

'But the main reason for coming was because Clara wanted to learn more about Dona Rosalía,' intervened Miguel. 'When she spoke to my grandmother, she was the one who told us to come here.'

'And what do they say at home about that corpse?' continued Sebastián, who seemed to ignore my friend's remarks.

'Not much,' I decided to be cautious, I still didn't know the reason for this second visit. 'They're pretty certain the body's been there since the war. They talk of a tall, young man under the age of thirty. But there's nothing to say who the body belonged to.'

Sebastián fell silent for a few minutes which seemed to last for ever, as if he'd forgotten our presence. Then he added:

'Who knows, it could be anyone. Especially bearing in mind servants were in charge of the manor house for several months. Pablo was at the front and his parents went to stay in Santiago. It must have been easy to hide a corpse you didn't want to be discovered. There was so much violence, so much settling of scores!'

'Perhaps you can tell us something about the body,' I ventured.

'No, love, no. How could I know anything? I spent most of the war in prison,' he glanced at Carme, who remained silent and attentive, as if her role were to act as a witness of that conversation. 'The thing is, I don't know why, I think about the body and the name of Rafael comes to my mind. Maybe because I know what happened to the other members of the party, those who died, those who escaped. But Rafael was never heard of again.'

'Well, you can set your mind at rest,' I commented. I wasn't going to tell him about the letters, Sebastián already knew everything in them, but I could at least confirm his suspicions were groundless. 'We found some documents which indicate Rafael left with the idea to reach Buenos Aires, just as you supposed.'

'I'm glad to hear that. Something must have happened to him during his escape, it's strange we lost track of him.'

'Perhaps he was killed before he got to Porto,' Miguel suggested. 'Gran told me the Portuguese police used to help Franco.'

'They did, but they'd capture the fugitives and return them to Spain. I imagine he was killed during his escape and his body abandoned in some gully or other. But that's something we'll never know for certain.'

'So don't you have any idea who the remains belong to?' I insisted. I had the impression Sebastián had called us to tell us something more than we already knew.

'I've been thinking a lot about that these days,' he replied. 'It could have been someone from Betanzos or Pontedeume, someone fairly well known. The Falangists murdered lots of people, but they never wanted to hide them, quite the opposite, they left them out by the roadside, so they would serve as a warning. But this one they may have wanted to keep secret.'

'And why would the Falangists use the manor, if there was no one there?'

Sebastián remained silent before my question, staring at the hills which were visible from the gallery. It was easy to see he was searching for the right words to tell us something important.

'They say you should never speak ill of the dead. But I'm not hurting your grandfather or anyone, these things took place too many years ago,' he continued after a while. 'Helping Rafael must have been Pablo's final act of generosity.'

'What do you mean?' I asked.

'All I know is what was rumoured in town, there was never any hard evidence. I couldn't know for myself, I spent all that time in prison. But it was said, after the first few weeks, Pablo took charge of the local repression.'

'The local repression? What's that?' asked Miguel.

'Pablo was the one who drew up the lists of those who had to be killed or punished. But he did it all from his office, he never got his hands dirty. He left that to Rosalía's oldest brother, Héctor, and his band. Héctor did get blood on his hands, he and his men committed every kind of atrocity you can imagine. If hell exists, I have no doubt he'll be burning in it now.'

'But my grandfather left for the front as soon as the war started, he almost wasn't here,' I objected, horrified by what I was hearing.

'He left, yes, but in the spring of 1937, once the region had been pacified, as they used to say. He came back a hero at the end of the war, with the rank of captain and covered with medals. Then, as mayor, he did whatever he felt like for years. Don't take it badly, Clara, but he ruined many people's lives. There's no point talking about it now, you can't change anything, but I thought you ought to know.'

'No one ever said anything about this at home,' I remarked sadly.

'As the years went by, these things became less important, we were all too busy trying to survive,' added Sebastián in a serious tone. 'Nobody talked about them, they were buried like that corpse you found. And they'll be buried even more once the few of us who are left have died.'

After all these years, I am convinced that parents are unknown to their children, since we tend to think life began, for them too, on the day we were born. In the case of grandparents, this ignorance is complete and irreversible. So it's not surprising I was amazed by all the things, none of them good, I was hearing about my grandfather Pablo.

'What about the skeleton?' I insisted, trying to retrieve the thread of our conversation.

'It could be anyone. As far as I'm aware, those responsible for the night outings had easy access to the manor.'

'The night outings?' I asked with the naivety of my sixteen years.

'The Falangists talked of "outings" when they took prisoners out to be killed. Bitter irony, I'm afraid. And to think those murderers carried on living here, among us! We had to put up with a lot.'

'So there's no way of knowing,' concluded Miguel, for whom Sebastián's memories must have been even more bitter, since they revived the pain his family had suffered.

'There is one possibility, which is why I called you here today. One of those responsible for the outings still lives in the town. You know the ironmonger's opposite the casino club? It's run by the son, but the one who set it up after the war was Demetrio: Demetrio Lamela, a murderer turned respectable citizen.'

'And you say he's still alive?'

'He is, he must be a couple of years younger than me. He was an associate of your grandfather's, I suppose he owed him many favours.'

'And you think he'd want to talk to us?' Miguel asked sceptically.

'Not to you, that's for sure. Nor should you talk to him, your grandmother wouldn't like it,' Sebastián answered quickly. 'But he might agree to talk to Clara, especially when he discovers she's Pablo Soutelo's granddaughter.'

19

It was still early when we left Sebastián's home. We both wanted to carry on our conversation, but we didn't want to be seen walking together in Vilarelle. So, at Miguel's suggestion, we took the track by the side of the house, descending through fields and vegetable gardens. It ended at the road which bypassed the town and we were then able to follow that back to the manor house.

On the way, we stopped next to a field of chestnut trees and sat under one of them. We immediately started discussing the meeting we'd just had.

'In the end, he didn't tell us anything we didn't know,' remarked Miguel after we'd gone over the information Sebastián had given us. 'We may even know more than he does.'

'My grandfather and that anonymous corpse could tell us something, but they're both dead.'

'Well, unless we conduct a seance and invoke the spirit of your grandfather...'

'Don't be dumb, this is serious!' I interrupted him and then added, 'There's still one thread we haven't pulled on: this Demetrio who came up at the end of the conversation. Why don't we pay him a visit?'

'You mean "you", you heard what the old man said. If things are as he suggested, he won't want to talk to me and

I don't ever want to set foot in that ironmonger's.'

Miguel's words struck me as reasonable. Besides, I remembered Sebastián had explained that the shop was opposite the casino club. If we went together, there was a good chance we would be spotted by one of the group of girls who were supposed to be my friends.

'Then I'll have to go on my own.'

'It's a good idea,' replied Miguel. 'Besides, this Demetrio will be chuffed to receive your visit. You're from the manor, he'll be proud to welcome you into his home.'

The following day, Ana was surprised and happy when I told her I would go with her to the casino club that afternoon. As I imagined, it was the perfect excuse and my mother was also delighted. So off I went with my cousin and for half an hour I played the role of a lady of leisure which Miguel hated so much, sitting outside and chatting with my friends. I left the first chance I had, I couldn't pass up such a good opportunity, and soon found the ironmonger's, a few buildings down on the other side of the street.

I went in. The shop was long and narrow, a little dark, with a wooden counter on the left which reached almost to the end. Behind the counter were shelves full of boxes. On the right, the wall was covered with more shelves, with a range of goods on display: earthenware and metal pots, pans, tins of paint, saws and scythes of various sizes, glass jugs and containers...

Behind the counter was a stout woman, her hair combed in a style which must have been fashionable twenty years earlier. She wore a floral dress and a blue woollen cardigan.

She was talking to a customer and showing him bulbs of different types and sizes. I waited for her to complete her sale. When the customer left, the woman came over to me.

'Can I help you?' From her look I had the impression she knew who I was, I suppose it was impossible for people from the manor to pass unnoticed in the town.

'I haven't come to buy anything,' I answered. Then, since she remained silent, I added, 'I was told I could find Demetrio Lamela here and I'd like to speak to him.'

'You're a Soutelo, aren't you?'

'I am, yes. My name's Clara. I'm Don Víctor's daughter.'

'Pleased to meet you. My name's Asunción,' she replied with a half-smile. 'Demetrio is my father-in-law. He's out the back, in the garden. If you wait here, I'll go and ask if he can see you.'

I thanked her and she disappeared through a door at the back of the shop. She came back after a while, with a broader smile on her face, and asked me to follow her. The door led to a short corridor which we walked down in silence. Another, glass door led to a small but very well tended garden. Apart from narrow paths which went from side to side, the whole of the earth was cultivated, divided into rectangular allotments, each devoted to a particular product: tomatoes, onions, peppers, potatoes, carrots, lettuces... Only the bottom of the garden had been left to grow wild, with some grass and three fruit trees. The tree on the right was an old-looking fig, under which was a wooden table and some chairs. One of these was occupied by an elderly man, who was sitting, reading the newspaper.

Asunción introduced us and then returned to the shop. I sat on another chair, opposite this Demetrio Lamela who, if Sebastián was to be believed, had been close friends with my grandfather. He was a slim man and looked of medium height when he got up to shake my hand. He had a thin moustache, a white line which stood out against his dark, weathered skin, criss-crossed by wrinkles. The little hair on top of his head was combed back, without any attempt to hide his bald patch. It was hard to believe that this old man had been one of those who murdered so many people locally. But I recalled Sebastián's words and felt a shiver run down my spine when I noticed the cold glint in his eyes.

'So you're Don Pablo's granddaughter, are you? A fine man, your grandpa. I knew him well, I was proud to be considered his friend.'

'I know, that's why I'm here. When we were talking about him at home, your name came up once or twice, as did references to your friendship.' It was a lie, of course, I'd never heard of him until our conversation with Sebastián, but I hoped my words sounded convincing. I decided to make the best of the opportunity in front of me to cut to the reason I was there, 'It's about my grandfather I wanted to talk to you.'

The man couldn't hide the satisfaction he derived from my words. The distrust disappeared from his face, to be replaced by an affable smile. It was obvious I couldn't have got off to a better start. Even so, he asked in a tone of surprise:

'But what can I tell you that your family doesn't already know?'

'The thing is I'm interested in my grandfather's story. I like to write and am working on a biography of him,' I improvised, hoping my lie sounded credible. 'My father, uncle and aunt have told me all they know, I have several tapes with recordings of their conversations. But I need to complete this information with testimonies from other people who knew him.'

'I knew him well, though I didn't have contact with him until the start of the war. We were in the same regiment, he was captain and I was sergeant. We soon hit it off. Your grandpa was an extraordinary person, I was honoured to be his friend,' Demetrio's voice sounded more confident, he must have felt he was walking on solid ground. 'After the war, when he was appointed mayor, I was one of his councillors, I stayed with him until 1959. He always held me in high esteem, it was a pleasure to be at his orders.'

I barely had to intervene for this man to string together anecdotes relating to Don Pablo, as he called him: battles at the front, harsh winters in Aragón, conquered cities, the task of setting up the new town council... Some of the things he told me were interesting, but had nothing to do with the reason I was there. I decided to be more direct in my questions.

'How was it when you went off to war? It must have been a terrible experience for you both.'

'It was hard, but necessary. Spain was in a bad state back then, which is why we had to go to war, there was no other option,' Demetrio's voice hardened again. 'Both Don Pablo and I were volunteers, we didn't wait to be called up. As he had an education, he went as an officer. I went as his adjutant, I already told you we spent the whole of the war together.'

'You said before as boys you didn't have any relationship. When did your friendship start then?'

'We first came into contact soon after the uprising began. You had to know back then who was your friend, and who wasn't. Don Pablo was a friend, no doubt about it.'

'I understand few people in Vilarelle sympathized with the Republic.'

'There weren't many of them, but they let themselves be known,' he replied sharply. It was clear he didn't like the way the interview was going. I decided to take a risk, in case he should suddenly bring it to a close.

'I was told about a schoolteacher who was friends with my grandfather, one Rafael. Did you know him?'

'Rafael? Yes, I knew him. But he wasn't from Vilarelle, he didn't stay here long.' Seeing I remained silent, he continued, 'That Rafael was a clever one. He left as soon as he could, went to Argentina, I think, and was never heard of again.'

'I suppose he left so he wouldn't be killed,' I ventured. 'I heard schoolteachers were killed, though I couldn't say why.'

'Well, I'll tell you,' replied Demetrio in a harsh tone which made me jump. 'They were mostly Reds, they were the ones who poisoned children, putting Communist ideas into their heads.'

'I also heard Republicans were put to death in the town. I think they called them outings,' I realized I was being provocative, but felt I had nothing to lose.

'Why do you ask that?' his words were full of suppressed rage. 'I thought you came to talk about Don Pablo.'

'I did. I ask because I heard things...'

'You heard things...' he interrupted me abruptly. 'Don't believe everything you hear, there are people intent on distorting the truth of what happened here during those years.'

'But I also read things,' I objected with a little fear. 'I read people were killed who...'

'People turned up dead, that's true, terrible things happen in war,' he interrupted me again. 'It might even have been the Reds killing each other; there was a settling of scores, though then they blamed us, Franco's forces.'

'Do you know if my grandfather was involved in any of this?'

'Don Pablo was an extraordinary man. An upstanding Spaniard and a real patriot,' answered Demetrio in a fury. He leaned forwards and his whole body became tense. For a moment, I thought he was going to slap me. 'About the rest, I can't remember. I'm old, my memory's not what it was, you'll have to forgive me.'

Having said this, he took the newspaper he'd left on the table and put it on his lap. He looked at me strangely; there was distrust in his eyes, but also a vein of hatred. This man wasn't going to say another word to me.

I quickly took my leave. I was frustrated at the outcome of the conversation, though now I think it was rather revealing. Back then I was still very young and didn't know that sometimes silence speaks louder than words.

20

$\mathcal{G}$oing by what I wrote in my diary, I can say that life continued as normal over the following days, the only things that happened not being of particular relevance to my story. From my mother's repeated attempts to talk to me (I suppose she'd noticed how my interests were changing and how I was growing more distant from her and Daddy) to the idiotic conversations I was forced to have with Ana, who'd split with her boyfriend and sought a shoulder to cry on at all hours of the day.

Some of the more pleasant aspects I recorded in my diary include the amazement I felt as I raced through the pages of *Moon Palace*, so different from anything I'd read until then. There was also a place for the friendly voice of Joe Strummer, which accompanied me day after day in the solitude of my bedroom. Also especially for my relationship with Miguel, which continued to take up the largest amount of space. A relationship which made me happy in every way and which was all the more interesting because of my father's prohibition, an obstacle we continued to get around with Carlos' secret help. I was in love, and the texts I wrote reflect this enthusiastic feeling I store in my memory like a treasure. To this sweet delirium was added the certainty that, through Miguel, I was discovering a side to life which had been closed to me, about which I knew little more than what I'd picked up in the many novels I read.

But now is not the time to discuss these things if I wish to continue with my story. I must, however, make reference to the entry for the twenty-second of August. That day I had a long conversation with my uncle, one of many we used to have in the evening in his room. I told him all about the second meeting with Sebastián and my visit to the ironmonger's. I felt discouraged since it was clear our investigations always led to a dead end. We could come up with all the hypotheses we wanted, but we still knew nothing about that anonymous corpse. Carlos, meanwhile, was intrigued by my news, especially by the conversation with Demetrio. I hadn't realized that what interested my uncle most was any information which enabled him to reconstruct the figure of his father, with whom he'd been at odds for many years of his life. It would take me several more years to understand this.

'I also have something to tell you,' said Carlos, having listened to my story. 'You remember the jar that was in the box, which my mother kept so secret? I gave it to Isabel, the coroner, so she could analyse the contents. And last night she rang me up to tell me the results.'

'What was in it?' I asked when Carlos remained silent in one of those theatrical pauses he was so good at. 'Come on, tell me!'

'The liquid in the jar turned out to be digoxin, a glycoside present in digitalis. You remember the plant you call Dead Man's Bells, the one with the purple flowers you like to pop? Well, its more common name is foxglove and you get digoxin from its upper leaves.'

'OK, that's enough of the science lesson! Why are the contents so important?'

'Because digoxin is a drug used in the treatment of heart conditions, especially in cases of heart failure. But it's a treatment with which you have to be very careful. Administered in small doses over too long a period, it accumulates and becomes toxic for the organism. The symptoms are obvious: increased heart rate, nausea, vomiting... Carry on, and in a few days it causes irreversible damage to the heart and normally ends in a heart attack.'

I didn't say anything. I couldn't see what importance all this detailed information might have. After a pause, Carlos continued in a serious tone:

'What I don't know is why my mother would want such a medicine, she never suffered from her heart, as far as I'm aware. What troubles me most is that she should hide it in that secret drawer; she obviously kept things there she didn't want others to see, including my father.'

'Why are you telling me all of this? What's so strange about it?'

'I'm telling you because my father died of a sudden heart attack. As far as I recall, he had a few complaints the days before, which seemed to have been caused by indigestion, but he didn't give it any importance. He never had problems, especially with his heart; quite the opposite, he always boasted he had the heart of a twenty-year-old. I know these things happen, anyone can have a heart attack, especially someone like that who didn't look after himself. But, having discovered this jar, I don't know what to think when I go over certain attitudes adopted by my mother.

Do you understand if I say associations come into my mind which frighten even me? I told you the last few years the two of them kept up appearances, I suppose because of us and the servants, but their relationship was increasingly distant. Mummy spent a large part of the day in her room, and Daddy grew increasingly irritable, was almost never at home.'

'Do you mean to tell me...?'

'I don't know what I mean, Clara,' my uncle interrupted me. 'I'm just saying what's in my head, it may be one of those obsessions which sometimes torment me. Anyone would think the appearance of this skeleton is driving us all mad, we see murder wherever we go.'

After dinner on the evening of the twenty-fourth of August, my father asked me to stay a little longer with them at the table. My uncle stayed as well, but Ana and the boys went to watch television. I was surprised by his request, since it was out of the ordinary, and also by the serious expression Daddy adopted when he spoke. He lit a cigar with slow movements, as he used to do when he was getting ready to say something important, and, having blown out the first smoke, asked me in a tense voice:

'Could you tell us what it is you're up to at the moment? I thought the warning I gave you about that mechanic would have sufficed, but now I see you're intent on spoiling the summer for all of us,' the silence of everybody at the table gave his words a hard edge. 'I would like to know what it is you're after, why you have to go about bothering people with your questions.'

'I don't know what you mean, Daddy,' I answered in an attempt to gain time so I could react better. Of course I knew exactly what he meant. I quickly realized someone had told him about my visit to the ironmonger's and also perhaps to Sebastián's house. If they'd told him this, he must know all about the nature of my questions.

'What is it? Have you acquired an interest in the elderly?' he continued in full flow. 'Why are you suddenly so concerned about the war, my father, and events which had long been forgotten before you were born?'

There was no point answering, it was clear he knew all about my conversation with Demetrio. Who had gone and told him, and why?

'Have you nothing to say? Elsewhere you seem to talk all the time. And where do you get all these ideas from? Not from that beggar, that trainee mechanic you're so fond of?'

My father had been gradually raising his voice. His face was flushed, the veins on his neck so pronounced I thought he might have a heart attack. He had those glaring eyes which always made me so afraid.

'Daddy's right,' my mother intervened in an attempt to fix something which was beyond repair. 'Holidays are for having fun, like Ana and her friends. You're young, you've plenty of people to go out with. And yet you insist on seeing that boy we know nothing about.'

Poor Mummy, I now think. All her life defending my father in an attempt to hold onto a fictitious happiness and peace, a make-believe happiness which was so important to her. I hated her that evening for her cowardice, for not daring to stand up for me, for not trying to understand my reasons, which wasn't so difficult. It was my uncle Carlos who stood up for me, having listened to my father's diatribe in silence.

'You're very unfair, Víctor, if you don't mind my saying so. You have an extraordinary daughter, more thoughtful and mature than most. More than you, that's for sure, don't be offended.'

'There's no need to come to her defence, Carlos, you're not the best example,' replied my father defiantly. 'You left home, forgot about our parents, led your life without a thought for family. What's to be expected of you?'

'One day, if you like, we'll go over how things were in our family, my vision is quite different from yours,' Carlos spoke slowly, though the indignation in his words was obvious. 'Or perhaps you lived with your eyes closed, paying attention only to what interested you. As you do now, by the way. You haven't changed one bit.'

'I'm not sure what you mean,' answered my father, surprised by the attack.

'Well, it's not difficult, Víctor. A corpse turns up in the house, with clear indications the person was murdered. And all you do is try to cover it up. You've no interest in finding out who the person was or who wielded the murder weapon. Am I to believe it's a simple lack of curiosity on your part?'

'Let bygones be bygones. What does any of this matter to us?' my father's face was again flushed and there was a rage in him I'd never seen before.

'Obviously it doesn't matter to you, but haven't you stopped to think the murderer may have lived in the manor?'

'That's saying a lot, there's no evidence.'

'The facts speak for themselves, I don't know what other evidence you need,' continued Carlos. 'That man you care nothing about was shot twice and then walled up. Here, in this house. It has something to do with us, don't you think?'

'All that's in the past. Are you not aware these events have prescribed?'

'What do I care if they've prescribed or not!' Now Carlos was the one raising his voice. 'I'm not talking here about legalities, I'm talking about a moral perspective, if you still know what that means.'

'Leave me alone, Carlos! Don't forget you're addressing me in front of my wife and daughter.'

'What's better, therefore – to ignore whatever happens? Maybe that's how you managed not to see Daddy's treatment of Mummy, you were always a specialist at looking the other way,' my uncle glanced at me and then back at my father. 'Well, the only thing that's happened is that Clara's not like you. It's that simple. Deep down, you should be pleased.'

The argument between them continued for quite a while, to my amazement and my mother's disappointment. They no longer raised their voices, but their words were like poisoned arrows, especially those of Daddy, who even raised the question of my uncle's homosexuality. I knew Carlos and Daddy were different, but I never imagined they could disagree like this. After all, they were brothers, they'd grown up together under the same roof. But that evening, rather than talking of me, what they seemed to be doing was settling scores with the past.

After a few minutes of stony silence, when the argument seemed to have reached an impasse, my father threw his final dart.

'I'm sorry to say this, Carlos, but the manor is mine now. If this is why you're going to come here, it would be better if you stayed in Barcelona. I'm getting old, I've just turned fifty. I have a right to enjoy everything I've achieved in life. And I'm not going to let anyone spoil that, be it my brother or my daughter. So now you know.'

And with that he got up from the table and headed for the stairs. Mummy waited a little longer, to ask for Carlos' forgiveness, the very next day Víctor would regret his harsh words. But she soon followed him upstairs, like an obedient servant.

My uncle and I were left staring at each other in silence, unable to put into words whatever it was we wanted to say. And so that dinner came to an end – a dinner which I can say, with the perspective of the years, may have been the first step in the decisions I would later have to take.

21

The following day, I didn't leave my room until the evening. The night before, I'd barely slept, my head hurt, as did my whole body, I didn't feel well. I had no wish to see my father, I couldn't bear the thought of being in the same room as him, nor did I want to sit at the same table as if nothing had happened. The person I really wanted to be with was Miguel, but that was impossible the way things were at home. I was afraid my uncle would pack his bags after the violent argument he'd had with my father, but he set my mind at rest by paying me a visit around midday: he planned to stay until the beginning of September, he didn't wish there to be an open wound in his relationship with his brother. And yet, though I may not have been able to express it clearly, it wasn't difficult to see that nothing would be the same again, since a rupture had appeared in our family.

Carlos' visit was the first of several I had that day, all of them important. They're all jotted down in my diary, so I can recall them here now with the security of knowing I won't fall into the traps set by memory. As well as coming to tell me he planned to stay a few more days, he was the bearer of news which left me feeling worried. Early that morning he'd received a call from a woman who identified herself as Miguel's mother. Her son had requested she phone the manor house, ask for Carlos and tell him that Miguel wanted to see him.

'Why didn't he call you himself? Why get his mother involved?' I asked, unsettled by this information.

'I don't know, Clara. I suppose he couldn't at that time, maybe they don't let him make calls from the garage,' answered my uncle in an attempt to calm me down. 'I agreed to stop by his house after lunch. When I'm back, I'll come and tell you what it was he wanted.'

The second important visit was from Celsa. My mother had popped in to see me and told her I wasn't feeling well and would prefer to have lunch in my bedroom. Around one o'clock, Celsa appeared with a tray with two battered hake pieces, some boiled rice, a yoghurt and fruit. I arranged myself in bed so I could eat a bit and, instead of leaving, she sat down next to me. After hesitating for a few moments, she said she had something to ask. I noticed she was nervous, as if she were afraid someone might come in and catch us together; there was also a note of mystery in her voice which intrigued me.

'My dad would like to talk to you, Clara. I don't know why, he wouldn't tell me. But he insisted you went to pay him a visit as soon as you could.'

'Your dad?' I asked in surprise. I made an effort to remember the person she was talking about, but no image came into my mind. I knew Celsa was married, her husband worked in the town hall and sometimes helped in the garden. I also knew her two children by sight, both of whom were older than me. They lived together in a house two hundred yards from the manor, a simple building with its own allotment behind. I passed in front of it on the way to town, but I'd never seen a man there as old as her father must be.

'My dad, that's right, he wouldn't let up until I promised I'd ask you. You probably don't remember him, he hasn't been well for years now and almost never leaves home. He has prostate cancer; until recently he still got by, he's one of those who can't sit idle. But he got worse at the start of the summer, I don't think he'll last long. He spends almost the entire day in bed. I try to get him up, but he always tells me to leave him alone, he hasn't much time left.'

'And why does he want to talk to me? He hardly knows me.'

'He remembers when you were little, he still came out then and did some gardening. Dad worked in the manor his whole life, from when he was a boy. Your grandparents were very fond of him, trusted him a lot.'

'I think I know who he is,' I said. I'd just conjured up the image of an older man cutting back the myrtles with some pruning shears. A man my grandmother had great respect for, I was sure it was him. 'But I still don't understand why he would want to see me.'

'He knows all about you. I always tell him what's going on in the house, he treats you as if you were family.' Celsa looked me in the eye and said, 'Last night I told him about the argument at dinner. I know it's none of my business, but in the kitchen you can hear everything that's said.'

'Don't worry, Celsa, you're one of us. What I still don't see is what last night's argument has to do with your father.'

'Something, that's for sure, because when I finished

telling him about it, he started asking me all sorts of questions about you.' Celsa gazed at me tenderly, in her face you could see the affection she had for me. 'I used to know you better, you don't talk to me so much now you've grown up, but I've a pretty good idea what kind of person you are. I told him you're more and more like Dona Rosalía, not just in your appearance. I mean you're noble and good. And you've a strong personality, you won't let yourself be bullied.'

I moved closer to Celsa and gave her a hug, I had only good memories of her. There she was, someone else who viewed me with affection. Like Miguel, like Carlos. How could I complain, how could I be sad, with people like that who loved me?

'Will you see him?' insisted Celsa when we'd let each other go. 'I wanted to tell him today, he'll ask as soon as I get back.'

'Tell him I'll be there tomorrow without fail. If you don't mind, you could come with me and introduce us. I'd also like to know what he has to tell me that's so important.'

At around six o'clock, Carlos came back into my room. I quickly noticed the look of concern and confusion on his face. I'd already got up and was sitting on the bed, leaning against the headboard. I knew he'd been to see Miguel and was immediately afraid, it was obvious something was not well.

'Miguel's not serious, don't worry,' said Carlos, as if he'd read my thoughts. He sat at the foot of the bed and continued, 'But he'll have to rest for several days. He has wounds all over his body, he shouldn't move until he's healed. He wanted to write you a letter, but I assured him I could tell you myself.'

'What happened to him? Did he have an accident in the garage?' A sudden knot of anguish had taken root in my stomach.

'No, Clara, I wish it was something like that. Miguel was beaten up yesterday evening. They gave him a good hiding, it was a professional job.'

I couldn't stop the tears pouring into my eyes. I cried, I cried in my uncle's embrace, as if my body couldn't endure the extra pain his words gave me. When I managed to calm down, Carlos went on:

'He finds it difficult to talk because his lips are swollen, but with what he told me I can give you a summary of what happened. Two strangers were waiting for him outside his house as night was falling. They put him in a car and drove him to a place called Dark Fountain, he said you'd been there together. They took him out of the car and started punching and kicking him. Quite thoroughly, given the result. They even threatened him with a gun, though I reckon that was just to frighten him. They left him there on the ground. He managed to make it to the main road, where he was lucky enough to be picked up by a lorry which brought him home. He's bruises all over his body, but nothing's broken. The doctor said rest and his natural constitution will soon make him better.'

'Who attacked him? Why would they do that?' What Carlos had just told me sounded more like a film than real life.

'That's the worst part, Clara. This attack on Miguel seems to have a lot to do with your visits, especially the visit you made to the ironmonger's. Because he said they threatened to beat him up more if he carried on sticking in his nose where it wasn't wanted. They told him to remember what had happened to his family during the war, if he didn't want to have to go through the same experience, and not to aim so high, the manor girl was a lot for him. I suppose by "manor girl" they meant you,' ended my uncle.

I was speechless, having listened to Carlos. My heart was oppressed, I felt like crying until I had no tears left, I was overwhelmed by a feeling of impotence. Apart from what had happened, I was struck by a sense of danger, the suspicion there may be people in town who still had reasons not to want the events of the war to come out.

I stared at Carlos. He was older than me, he had experience of life and I trusted him more than anyone, so I asked him if he knew what we should do.

'I would say nothing. Miguel's mother doesn't want to report this to the police, she's obviously very afraid. She may know things about the town we don't. Don't forget the families of those who lost the war lived with the consequences for many years.' Carlos pondered for a little before going on, 'As for what I think, I have a few ideas. It seems clear someone knows about your visits, it must be difficult in this town to escape notice. It's also pretty obvious this person is particularly annoyed about your visit to the ironmonger's.'

'That Demetrio, what a wretch! He's the only one who could have said something. Sebastián was right, he's not to be trusted.'

'All he had to do was tell his son or daughter-in-law. Then they'll have told someone else, it's the only way to explain this attack on Miguel.'

'But why? We haven't done anything wrong!'

'As I see it, you made a few people nervous. They must have wanted to warn you they're not going to allow you to keep digging around. Now we know what methods they use. I suppose they left you alone because you're a girl and, above all, because you're a Soutelo. So they contented themselves with telling your father, perhaps asking him to solve the problem with you directly.'

'Do you think Daddy could have...?'

'I don't have a good opinion of my brother, you know that. But I don't think he's capable of arranging for Miguel to be beaten up. I'm pretty sure, though, that he knows those who could have done it.'

'But who? You talk about people who content themselves, who are capable... But who are they?'

'I can't answer you that, Clara. I don't know. But I know what my duty is, not only as your uncle, but as someone who loves you. Leave this matter alone, persuade Miguel as soon as he's better. I think we already know quite a lot, enough to be sure your father wants to cover up the skeleton not just to preserve the family's good name. There are other reasons.'

'What are they?'

'Do you really care? We could find out, it wouldn't be that difficult to learn who's really in charge in this town. But I don't think we'd gain anything by doing so.'

'Are we going to let them get away with it?' I protested.

'I'd say we're going to avoid the nest of vipers before they get angry and pick a fight. You did well, we already know a lot. I think the time has come to remind you of what my mother said when I finished university.'

'And what was that?'

'One day when we were alone, she advised me, "Leave here as soon as you can, you've still time. You're not like them. Don't let them turn you into another Soutelo." That's what she said to me, the same as I'm telling you now. You're still young, you'll have to wait a bit. But escape from here as soon as you have the chance, you can always rely on my help. What do you think about studying for a degree in Barcelona?'

'I've a long time to wait before that happens. What do I do until then?' Despite my confusion, I was aware Carlos' words made a lot of sense. He'd caught me by surprise, but he was offering me an exit which suddenly appeared very attractive.

'The time goes faster than you think. Meanwhile, patience and cunning, dear niece. It's the best advice I can give you.'

That was the day of hugs. After this intense conversation, I also hugged my uncle and, through him, Miguel. They were the only two people I could completely trust. Outside my room, a hostile world was waiting for me and I had no choice but to return. Life would carry on and I couldn't allow myself to be defeated. In the future, I would have to use patience and cunning, just as my uncle had recommended.

22

At eleven o'clock the following morning, Celsa came to fetch me from my room. She had to go to town to buy some cake tins, so now was a good time to take me to her house. I quickly got changed, I was eager to know what this strange man had to tell me. We soon arrived, I already said they lived nearby. The only person at home was her father, who was lying in one of the back rooms. When we entered, the blinds were almost completely closed, casting the room into shadow so that we could barely see.

Celsa raised the blinds halfway and light poured into the room. I then saw that the bedroom was small with just the necessary furniture: a bed, a night table, a chest of drawers, an armchair with various cushions. There was a built-in wardrobe which occupied the whole of the wall next to the door. Lying in bed was a man who looked extremely old, especially since he hadn't shaved. He was very slight with thin hair and sunken eyes. There was an air of confusion about him, like that of someone who's lost.

When he saw us come in, he tried to sit up. He was wearing a grey T-shirt with the words 'New York University' written in green letters, I imagined it must belong to one of his grandchildren. Celsa placed two cushions next to the headboard, which he leaned against. His name was Vicente, this was the first thing he told me when I greeted him.

He stared at me with curiosity, I suppose he was trying to see in me features which reminded him of the little girl he'd once known.

'So you're the Clara my daughter's always talking about. Celsa's right, you do look more and more like Dona Rosalía.'

I smiled and accepted a compliment I'd heard so often it was beginning to sound familiar. I then sat down in the armchair and waited for this man to tell me what he had to say. But first he addressed his daughter:

'Off you go, Celsa, attend to your own affairs. What I have to tell Clara here is for her ears only.'

I could see Celsa wasn't pleased by her father's words. She made as if to object, but then seemed to accept the situation. She said she'd be an hour doing her errands and would come to pick me up. With that she left. When he heard the sound of the door closing, Vicente asked me to move closer to his bed.

'We don't have much time, Clara, so I'm not going to beat about the bush. I have something important to tell you, as you've probably guessed.'

'Why me? I mean you hardly know me.'

'I know more than you might think, from what Celsa's told me. I may be wrong, but it's a risk I must take. I think you're the only one from the manor I can trust with my secret.'

He lowered his voice, so I had to lean towards him to hear better. I had the impression he found it tiring to voice the words, as if he were waging a constant battle with an illness which stole the little energy keeping him alive.

After a pause, he continued:

'A very big secret. I'm old and I'm very ill, it won't be long before I die, and I do not want to take this to the grave with me. I already told the priest in confession, I should feel relieved, having made my peace with God. But it's not enough, I can't leave with such a burden.'

He stopped talking, as if he found it difficult to make up his mind. His agitated breathing was the only sound in the silence of his room. We stayed like that for several minutes until he started speaking again:

'Please try to understand me. When death is so close, you see life differently. Things which seemed important are no longer so. And others you made an effort to forget turn into obsessions. Like this secret of mine.'

Until that point I had been mildly interested without giving it too much importance. But Vicente's last words filled me with tension, there was so much anguish in them. I suddenly realized this was one of those rare moments when life seems to condense and demands our utmost attention.

'I swore Don Pablo I'd never say a thing, but I don't think I'm breaking my promise by telling you too. He's died, as has Dona Rosalía, there's almost nobody left from those years. It can't harm anyone if you know. All I ask is that you make good use of what I'm going to tell you. I don't think Don Víctor or Dona María should ever know. Or Don Carlos, there's no point causing unnecessary hurt.'

I nodded. Questions were piling up inside me, but there was no way I was going to break the flow of Vicente's story.

'I started working in the manor in the spring of 1929, I shall never forget. I was very young, barely fifteen, but back then at that age you had to work like a man. Don Pablo wasn't much older than me, which may have been why he took to me from the beginning, relied on me for everything. I was the servant and he was the lord of the manor's son, but in our own way we were very fond of each other.

'In 1936 war broke out. Don Raimundo and Dona Carme moved to Santiago at the start of August, they didn't want to be here while so much was going on and nobody was safe. Don Pablo and I were left in the manor alone. The maids were here too, but we were the only ones who slept in the main building. I slept in the storeroom downstairs, where I'd set up a bed.

'It took me a while to realize something funny was going on. I didn't use to go upstairs, but one night I saw Don Pablo coming down from the attic with an empty pot in his hands. I didn't say anything, one of my virtues was knowing when to keep quiet, but from that day on I began to observe details I might otherwise have overlooked.

'I suspected there was someone else in the manor house, someone my master was hiding, there was no other explanation. This became more obvious after a few days when the mystery person moved into the room next to Don Pablo's, a small room which was always closed. I knew because the lights in both rooms stayed on until late, a detail no one outside the manor would have noticed. My master and his companion used to talk until the early hours of the morning. I sometimes had to cross the corridor and would hear the murmur of conversations, normally in Don Pablo's room. But they spoke in low voices you could barely make out.

'It was at that time Don Pablo's mood underwent an obvious change, as if he'd suddenly grown bitter. He sometimes addressed even me rudely, when before he'd always been polite. I put it down to the tensions war had brought to the town, not a morning went by without a corpse turning up at the roadside. It never occurred to me to think the reason could be the mysterious occupant of the room, even though I had seen the night conversations often turned into angry arguments which could be heard through the wall and in the corridor. So it was I made out references to the war, people who'd turned up dead, the Falangists... But the name which kept cropping up was that of Dona Rosalía, a single girl at the time my master was keen on, though she didn't pay him much attention.

'One night around the middle of August, there was a real racket coming from the room, bigger than usual. Voices were raised, as in a heated discussion, which continued for quite some time and only stopped when there was a dull sound, as of a bullet. I immediately got up, I was always on the lookout back then for what might happen. Shortly after that, Don Pablo came to get me. He was out of sorts, I'd never seen his face so contorted, though he made an effort to maintain his composure. He said there was a dead man upstairs and he needed my help. I went up with him. The corpse was lying on the carpet in the bedroom, with lots of blood, especially around the head. I knew that man, everybody in the town knew him. His name was Rafael, he'd been sent as a schoolteacher barely a year before. There was no doubt he was the mystery guest who'd shared the manor house with us during the previous weeks.

'I was greatly surprised, I could have imagined it was anyone other than the schoolteacher, my master had only disparaging comments to make about him. I didn't know what had happened between them that night, though it wasn't difficult to surmise. Nor did I ask – what was I going to say? It was enough to follow Don Pablo's orders, I already said I was very loyal to him. He wanted me to help him get rid of the corpse. "Not bury it in the garden or wood, they always end up being discovered," he said. He spoke in a dry, mechanical tone; he'd recovered from his initial confusion and was again in control of the situation. "Listen to what I have to say: this man was never here, you never saw him with me, he never entered the manor. Understand, Vicente? That's why he now has to disappear for ever."

'It was then I came up with an idea for getting rid of the body. I'd been working downstairs for several days, dividing an open space into smaller rooms. My plan was simple: to create a false partition wall and put the body inside the gap. "Wall it up" was the phrase Don Pablo used.

'So that's what we did. We wrapped it in the carpet and carried it downstairs. I built two walls, working the whole night through, without resting for a minute. When I'd finished plastering the walls, there was nothing to be seen: that corpse would remain hidden for ever, its presence ignored. Don Pablo made me promise to keep silence until the day I died. We never spoke about the events of that night again, the order was to forget it.

'That's what I did. I kept my word, I never told anybody. Until today, when I'm telling you. I never stopped feeling remorse, which grew in me with every year. I can't go to the other world with a secret like this, it's enough for Don Pablo to have done so. Especially when I know the body's finally turned up after so many years. It's true that nothing's eternal; except for death, there's no coming back from that.

'I realize you've been asking questions. Celsa is aware of your comings and goings. You do well, you've a right to know. I don't wish to give you the burden I've been carrying, it's up to you to decide who else should know about it. Just be careful who you tell, it's not worth ruining anyone's life. And I would ask you not to tell my daughter, she shouldn't hear a word of this.'

Having completed his long confession, Vicente fell back, finally free of the tension which had kept him upright while he was talking. He murmured 'thank you' several times in a thin voice; the narrative had left him exhausted. I remained silent for a few minutes, watching him, without knowing what to say. I suppose I should have asked him more questions, learned details only he could tell me. I've thought about it a lot, I lost an opportunity to clear up a mystery I can still only glimpse at today. But I didn't do this, I was too impressed by what I'd heard. A revelation which answered all the questions occupying my mind since the start of the summer.

A little later, we heard the sound of the door and Celsa came in. She found the two of us in silence, staring at each other, just as she'd left us. She didn't say anything either, I imagine she was dissuaded by the serious expression on my face. She covered her father, who'd retreated under the blankets, and replaced the cushions on the armchair. I got up, ready to leave. As I was going out, I heard Vicente's thin voice one more time:

'After that, Don Pablo changed a lot, he was never the same. And when he got married, the person I was always loyal to was Dona Rosalía. Now there's someone who was good.'

I left in Celsa's company. I knew I would never see that man or enter that house again. I also knew I would never forget the time I'd spent there, the revelations I'd heard were too important. Not because they answered the questions Miguel and I, and also Carlos, had been asking ourselves since the start of the summer, they didn't matter. His words were important because they shed a different light – a harsher, crueller, more intense light – on all my family history. That's why they affected me so much. Because the waves of a crime committed so long before had reached me as well, though I still didn't realize with what force they were going to hit me.

23

At the end of August, my aunt María and her husband César returned from a long trip around the Mediterranean on a friend's yacht. The fact there were more people in the manor helped me lead a more independent life. I stopped going to town, I felt aversion towards everybody after what had happened to Miguel. I again spent long periods alone in the mirador, with the sensation the summer was coming full circle. Other times I shut myself in my room, absorbed in my reading or letting the hours go by without doing anything, aware this strange summer was coming to an end and we would soon have to return to the routine of the city.

I suppose we don't realize the importance of certain periods in our life until much later. I reread the notes in my diary referring to those days and they strike me as poor and superficial. They never hint at the consequences those two months would have. Perhaps because, as I said, I only wrote down external facts and omitted the heap of conflicting sentiments bubbling away inside my head.

I shared Celsa's father's secret with my uncle and Miguel, it was too much weight for me to carry alone, though I didn't reveal the name of the person who'd told me. It didn't matter, that was not the important thing. After all, I don't suppose it would have been difficult for someone like Carlos to guess.

When I spoke to my uncle, who'd been away for two days on a trip to the Serralves Museum in Porto, he was so amazed it took him some time to react. He gazed into the distance for several minutes, as if instead of being in my room he were somewhere else, lost in his memories. 'A murderer's son,' he kept repeating with his head in his hands, like a mantra. 'A murderer's granddaughter,' I suppose I could have said, though I kept quiet. When Carlos managed to recover, we launched into a conversation which helped us to try and order all this new information.

'I have lots of doubts, we'll never know if it was a spontaneous or premeditated act. Or whether Daddy killed him because of political or romantic differences. Or a combination of both,' said Carlos at one point in our conversation. 'Perhaps it's better not to know for sure, I don't think I could take it.'

'Why do you say that?'

'Because if I think about it coldly, I find only cruelty in my father's behaviour. To betray a friend like that, to draw him into the manor and end up killing him. With Rafael out of the way, he was free to conquer my mother. It's terrible to think that, if it was deliberate, his plan worked to perfection.'

My uncle maintained Grandma Rosalía must have had her suspicions, even known about it at some stage. It was obvious she'd never forgotten Rafael, she kept the photos and letters in a secret place. Had she really discovered the role her husband had played? We could never be certain, though Carlos had a theory about when this could have happened. He told me the first year he'd gone to study in

Santiago, his parents had stopped sleeping together and Grandma Rosalía had moved into the bedroom where I'd always known her, the place I found the photos. Something must have made her take this decision to end her marriage even if they kept up appearances. But this was another detail which would remain forever veiled in mystery.

What Carlos didn't dare put into words, though he hinted at it several times, was the suspicion Grandma Rosalía provoked my grandfather's death, cleverly carrying it out using the medicine she kept in the wooden box. Was this to avenge Rafael's murder or to free herself of a husband who made her life unbearable? Again we would never know, there are some things in the past which are beyond our reach. And though I never said this to Carlos, I had another doubt: how much of this did my own father know or suspect? Was this the real reason he was so intent on covering up Rafael's skeleton, rather than the excuse he gave of safeguarding the family name? These were all unanswered questions.

On the twenty-eighth of August, I went to see Miguel at home. He was still in bed, but looked a lot better than my uncle had described him. His mother and grandmother were obviously concerned, I'm not even sure they were happy about my visit. They may have thought that I was ultimately to blame for what had happened, and they wouldn't have been entirely wrong. To start with, his mother stayed in the room, as if she didn't want to leave us alone. In the end, Miguel had to ask her to go, after a few moments of casual conversation.

When we were finally alone, we kissed and embraced with urgency, we hadn't been together for days and both wanted to feel the other's body. His lips were still swollen, but I suppose he liked my kisses more, because he didn't complain.

It was that afternoon I shared with him all the new information I possessed, including some of my uncle's suspicions. 'It's a secret,' I said, 'neither your mother nor your grandmother should know.' He was also surprised when he learned the circumstances of Rafael's death, together with my grandmother's possible act of vengeance, which he took to be true. That said, deep down he wasn't that amazed, my news went hand in hand with his vision of the world. 'Rich and poor, conquerors and conquered. History is always the same,' I remember he said at one point in our conversation. 'You manor people will always be manor people.'

'They will be,' I corrected him, 'don't include me in the same group. Remember what I told you once: nobody chooses the family they're born into.'

We saw each other over the following days, but outside, since he now felt better and began to lead a normal life, though he didn't go back to his work in the garage. I remember the last days of the month I concentrated almost exclusively on my relationship with Miguel, I didn't care about my father's prohibition. On the thirty-first, we went back to the river, to Charming Rock, which had become our secret hideaway. It was another evening of kisses and caresses, another night of shooting stars bursting inside me. I returned home late, very late, and got another severe telling-off from my father. But I didn't mind listening to him, I wasn't paralyzed by his threatening look, I never would be again. What I did was remain silent, for the first time I put my uncle's recommendations into practice. It was then I knew my life was entering a different phase in which nothing would be the same.

The fourth of September is the last date I wrote down in my diary that summer. My parents had decided to extend the holidays for a few more days, owing to the excellent weather we were having, and this coincidence made it possible for me to attend Rafael's funeral. Carlos found out about it from his friend Isabel. The case remained formally open, but the judge had decided the remains found in the manor house, which as far as justice was concerned were as anonymous as on the first day, should be laid to rest in the municipal cemetery.

Vilarelle cemetery is located outside the town and lacks the charm of old country graveyards. There was another one next to the main square, with ancient vaults and tombs, but no one had been buried there for years. The new one was a cold and impersonal rectangular space criss-crossed by cement alleyways, its walls covered with rows of niches, which from a distance looked like strange apartment blocks. In one of these niches, located close to the ground, two employees from the undertaker's placed a simple coffin containing the bones of the skeleton. As well as the judge, the coroner and another two people who must have come as witnesses, the only ones who attended the cold ceremony were Miguel, my uncle and me.

I imagined, for the judge and others, that morning was just another bureaucratic act, a tiresome engagement they cared little about, which formed part of their duties. I later found out I was wrong, there only needed to be one witness and the two funeral employees, the judge and coroner rarely attended such acts. Isabel had wanted to accompany my uncle, but I still don't know what brought the judge to the cemetery. Had my father asked him to go? Was he curious about an unsolved murder? I never learned the truth of this.

I do know, however, that they were burying the remains of a dead man without a name, whereas for the three of us it was an important ceremony, we were burying someone we wanted in some small way to make amends to. For us, he did have a name, even if we lacked other biographical data, and a life we'd learned enough about to feel it very close to ours. Rafael had been friends with Miguel's great-grandfather and great-uncle, he'd shared with them a time of hope, the ideals of a better, fairer society. And above all he'd been my grandmother Rosalía's love, they might even have got married had that atrocious war not turned everything upside down. He was also the man my grandfather had murdered, in a perfect crime which had somehow escaped the clutches of time.

It was a sad funeral, a sadness which was increased by the sky, full of grey clouds which pointed to autumn. There I was, with Miguel on one side and my uncle on the other, while they positioned the granite slab and then sealed the joins with cement. Before leaving, I'd plucked a few roses from the manor gardens and made a quick bouquet, which

I placed in front of the niche, on the plaque with no names or dates. A few drops of colour to liven up the drabness of the stone.

This was the last act of homage to someone who, from the depths of time, had helped to radically change my life. His bones had left the darkness of his strange tomb at the start of the summer and returned to the niche's obscurity at the summer's close. They'd been in the light for barely two months, but they'd had a dramatic impact on us. The three of us were aware that, in those few weeks of our lives, we hadn't just rescued Rafael's memory from the jaws of oblivion. He too, with his mute presence, had been like a stone which as it falls disturbs the still waters of a pool, provoking a succession of ripples which end up affecting the whole surface, as they affected me, shaken to the core by the events of that unforgettable period.

24

I must round off my story. Nothing else happened that summer, though in life it did. Life always follows its course without paying attention to the arbitrary limits we attempt to impose on it. We returned to Coruña, to the same routine as every winter. I started the last two years of school, trying to follow Carlos' recommendations. I grew increasingly distant from my parents, who seemed to resign themselves to my behaviour, which they didn't understand. They put it down to adolescence, the crises of youth, and I did nothing to correct them. There was no way they could guess it went deeper than that; they didn't know what I knew, they couldn't even imagine.

Those were very hard years for me. Circumstances obliged me to grow up fast, but perhaps I didn't have the necessary age or maturity to deal with such an adverse situation. Suppressing all I knew, not letting the hidden part of the iceberg carry me away, living with my family, which, especially in the case of my father, I found unbearable. And the loneliness, the radical sense of loneliness, despite being surrounded by people for most of the day. Those were hard years, as I said, and there they are, etched in my memory.

Miguel's letters, and those of Carlos, helped me to survive. I abandoned my diary, all I have from that period is a few, scribbled notes. I preferred to write to people I loved, to know someone was reading the only genuine sentiments I was able to express back then. I wrote to them all through those two years, they were the hands which held me up during the long months of my inner exile.

The following two summers, I didn't return to Vilarelle. I spent them abroad with my family's approval and the excuse that I needed to improve my English. The first year I was in London, thrilled by the experience of being in a foreign country, free for the first time of my parents' watchful gaze. I spent the second summer on a farm somewhere in the plains of Illinois, with a family who took me in as part of an immersion programme. It was a necessary experience which taught me how to live with loneliness. I have indelible memories from those months, the immense cornfields stretching into the distance or the unusual sight of thousands of glow-worms filling the air, illuminating the night with their phosphorescent beams.

When the time came to start university, I decided to study literature and art history at Barcelona's Autonomous University. My parents' dismay was memorable, they had other plans for me, but I refused to budge. I was legally an adult and had Carlos' financial and moral support. For a few months I lived in his house, where I finally met Andreu and began a friendship which, with Carlos gone, continues firm and active today. I later became independent and shared various flats with friends I made as I settled into my new surroundings.

My uncle came to an agreement with Miguel which I only found out about later on. He offered him what could only be considered an unusual grant, to cover the cost of the studies he chose to undertake. Carlos' proposal may have been born of a wish to help my friend escape what looked like a fixed destiny, or of guilt for being a descendant of the Soutelos, I cannot say. And so, in his spare time, Miguel went through secondary school and then did a degree in journalism at Santiago University.

We carried on seeing each other several times a year, on the brief visits I made to the house in Coruña, but our adolescent love faded away. Because of time, or distance, or simply because this was the way it had to be, life was calling us in different directions. The love and passion faded away, but not our friendship. Our friendship continued to grow with us. He's now editor on a newspaper in Vigo and the rest of the time he devotes himself to photography. His work is original and good, he doesn't hide his non-conformist view of life. He's happy and doing well. He's still my best friend, the person I call when life hits me and I need a place to take shelter.

Life's blows... Some have been symbolic, like the death of Joe Strummer in December 2002. The voice which kept me company in those decisive years has gone for good, but I still have the consolation of his records. There were other, harsher blows of the type life seems to choose in order to test us. The last one was Carlos' death about a year ago. I was already working in his publishing house, having finished my studies, so I owe him most of my professional experience as well. He was always my closest support, my second father. I could still have the benefit of his affection, and all he taught me about life, had a stupid accident on one of his frequent trips not deprived us of his intelligence and companionship.

When the will was read out, we discovered Carlos had foreseen such an eventuality. He left his galleries to Andreu and the publishing house to me. He also left us both the treasure he kept on his computer, the text he'd worked on over the years, a lucid and uncompromising account of the circumstances in which he'd lived. *Memory of Me* was the title he gave it in his will, where he made it clear he wanted only the two of us to read it.

In the publishing house, we went to great lengths to prepare a special edition with a very low print run: two sole copies, one for Andreu and one for me. Every now and then I reread the pages of this exceptional book and return to the notes of that summer, which often make reference to me and my naive search for the meaning of life.

I pay special attention to the text Carlos placed at the start of his book. It's a quote from James Joyce, an author he greatly admired, taken from his book *A Portrait of the Artist as a Young Man*:

I will not serve that in which I no longer believe, whether it call itself my home, my fatherland, or my church: and I will try to express myself in some mode of life or art as freely as I can and as wholly as I can, using for my defence the only arms I allow myself to use – silence, exile, and cunning.

Exile, yes, I shall never return to Vilarelle. But not silence. Whenever we recalled that summer which was so important to me, Carlos would always say, 'Tell it, tell it when you feel you have the necessary strength and ability. Don't let it fade away, as if they were just useless memories.'

Many years have gone by, but here is the text I finish today. In a way, it's another open tomb. In it, Rafael was waiting. He never received legal recognition, the case was filed away as my father wanted. It doesn't matter now. The important thing is that he lived on all these years in my memory, and will carry on doing so in these pages. Let this text of mine be the silent cry of the Rafael my grandmother loved and all those who have loved and dreamed in times of hardship, letting themselves be led by the life force which beats inside every human being. The one I feel beating in me, which gave me the incentive to come this far.

Acknowledgements

The composition of a novel is always a long and arduous journey, with solitude as principal companion. But there are also friendly voices which offer company and help, and which end up being essential so that you can reach the end. Which is why I would like to acknowledge here all those who helped me through this process.

Montse Paz and Manuel Bragado let me pillage their library in search of the books I needed to learn about the architecture of Galician *pazos* or manor houses and the circumstances in Galicia of the Spanish Civil War. Antonio Reigosa of Lugo's Provincial Museum gave me very useful information about the houses I was particularly interested in. The lawyer Xulio Villarino advised me on legal questions, while the coroner José Antonio Sampayo did the same on questions relating to his profession. In addition, they both agreed to read a draft of the novel and to point out any errors. My daughter, Mariña, as well as being with me in the busy, exciting days I spent planning this novel, gave me very useful advice about the Clash and other rock bands.

Bernardo Máiz and María Carmen Bar shared valuable insight into some of the more important aspects of history. They both appeared as fictional characters in one of the chapters in the draft novel, which was finally left out (because, as in films, we authors are sometimes obliged to sacrifice bits in the final product, with the disadvantage that, unlike with DVDs, there's no way of including them as bonus features). All the same, their hidden presence can be detected in many pages.

Isabel Soto's constant support during the writing of this book was very important to me. I owe her and Manuel Bragado a careful reading of the first draft and the valuable suggestions they both made. I am also grateful for words of encouragement to Miguelanxo Prado and Uxía López Meirama, who were enthusiastic about the original idea. And how to forget the help of Xavier Senín, who lent me his computer so that I didn't have to stop working for several weeks? Finally, Dolores Torres París, with her detailed revision, helped give the text its final form.

Special thanks are due to Dinah Washington, as alive today as she was when she recorded some magnificent albums in the 1950s. Those albums – *For Those in Love* most of all – formed the main part of the soundtrack which kept me company during the long hours I spent writing this book.

Read more titles in the series  published by Small Stations Press!

Agustín Fernández Paz, WINTER LETTERS

I pick up my pen in the hope that searching for the exact words to explain today's events might help me understand what has happened. Because, dear Xabier, I don't know what to think or do any more. Now I'm really, really afraid. The best thing to do at the moment would be to leave this house, abandon everything, return to Berlin and merge once more with the calming din of Alexanderplatz. Because it's true until yesterday I was a bit scared, but what was happening was simply a game between that strange book and me. A game in which I felt, despite everything, I remained in control of the situation. Now that's all changed, I can't go back after what's happened today. How can I leave her alone? How can I ignore her plea for help?

'The oldest and strongest emotion of mankind is fear, and the oldest and strongest kind of fear is fear of the unknown,' writes H. P. Lovecraft at the start of his essay *Supernatural Horror in Literature*. In real life, the author Agustín Fernández Paz, Galicia's answer to H. P. Lovecraft, is reading the newspaper and comes across a classified ad for a haunted house. He imagines what would happen if someone answered that ad. Then what would happen if they went to see the house and liked it. Then what would happen if they had enough money and decided to buy it. And finally what would happen if they went to live there and discovered that the house was really haunted. This is the plot of *Winter Letters*, one of the best-selling Galician novels of all time. The house will bring to mind, for older readers, the Bates' home in Alfred Hitchcock's film *Psycho*. Inside the house is a book of prints that may remind younger readers of Tom Riddle's diary in *Harry Potter and the Chamber of Secrets*. However this may be, the reader is sure to be drawn in by the force and power of the narrative, which is as smooth and sinuous as the sirens' song heard by Ulysses from the sanctuary of the mast of his ship.

ISBN 978-954-384-041-0

Agustín Fernández Paz, BLACK AIR

Had I remained silent, had I concealed my interest at that point, I might now be in a completely different situation, far away from the horror that has been ceaselessly gnawing away at me for the past three years. And yet my words simply paved the way for what Dr Montenegro had to say:

'You will learn more about Laura Novo, Dr Moldes. She is going to be your first patient. Under my supervision, of course. You have new ideas, you may be the only person capable of shedding light on a case that has kept the rest of us in the dark. I know it's not an easy challenge, but perhaps, with your passion for knowledge, you're the only one who can find a solution that goes beyond the boundaries of accepted practice. I'll have her case history sent to you at once. Good luck, Víctor, my friend, and welcome to Beira Verde Clinic!'

Víctor Moldes is an outstanding psychiatry student, looking to test his knowledge on patients. He is given a job at the prestigious Beira Verde Clinic in Galicia, near the Portuguese border, and handed a patient, Laura Novo, who is capable only of writing her name on blank sheets of paper. Slowly he draws her out of herself and she agrees to tell him her story, how she left Madrid in order to work on her thesis and escape a difficult relationship that was going nowhere. Her return to the land where she grew up, to stay in a guest house run by a schoolteacher she had fallen passionately in love with when she was a teenager, has fatal consequences. Her presence in the remote area of Terra Chá awakens the Great Beast, who up until that moment had been slumbering in the depths of the earth. Once awake, the Great Beast has one year to achieve its objective. Dr Moldes finds himself drawn into a conflict he is barely able to understand, let alone control, and, having finally pieced together the fragments of the narrative, he is in a race against time to save his patient.

ISBN 978-954-384-028-1

Ledicia Costas, HEART OF JUPITER

Isla had often thought that her destiny was written in the stars. As if it didn't matter what kind of decisions she took. The influence of the heavenly bodies was so strong that, in the end, her fate would always be fulfilled. There was no way of avoiding what had been drawn in the map of the sky at the beginning of time.

A gust of cold wind brushed past her thoughts and gave her goosebumps. She said goodbye to Mar, went back in the house and straight to her room.

Out of habit, she picked up the laptop. She had a message in her inbox.

'Jupiter,' she murmured, her heart beating faster.

She placed the cursor over the message and opened it.

By the winner of the 2015 Spanish National Prize for Children's and Young Adult Literature, *Heart of Jupiter* is the story of a teenage girl, Isla, who moves home and has to start over at a new school in Region. Here she makes friends with Mar, who helps her adjust to her new circumstances, but she also comes across Oak, who is determined to make her life miserable and seems to bear a grudge. She spends her nights chatting online with Jupiter. They share a common passion for the stars. Isla finds solace in their relationship, but Mar remains unconvinced and would prefer to see Isla in a relationship with Anxo, a boy from their school, someone she has actually seen. Isla is insistent, however: Jupiter and she have arranged to meet on Midsummer's Eve, when they will finally discover whether their online relationship is for real...

ISBN 978-954-384-049-6

Elena Gallego Abad, DRAGAL II: THE DRAGON'S METAMORPHOSIS

'About fifty years ago, towards the start of the 1960s, an old priest on his deathbed gave his deacon a wooden box, charging him never to open it... until he received a sign from the stone statue affixed to the façade of St Peter's. He then revealed that he belonged to a secret order whose duty it was to protect a dragon's magic and prepare its return to life.'

'A knight of the Order of Dragal!'

'The task didn't seem all that difficult. He should never open the box or mention it to anybody... All he had to do was wait for signs that would herald the fulfilment of a thousand-year-old prophecy.'

'Have you been waiting all this time?'

Father Xurxo nodded...

In this second instalment of the saga by Elena Gallego Abad devoted to the Galician dragon Dragal, the schoolboy Hadrián, who with his friend Mónica discovered the dragon's remains in the catacombs under St Peter's Church, is locked in a struggle with the dragon to see who will come out on top. Mónica has promised to take some food to the Moor's Pool, where her friend has gone for refuge, but is unsure what dragons eat when they're not devastating the local population. Before setting out, however, she receives strange, handwritten messages of warning, telling her not to go. She seeks help — first from the parish priest, Father Xurxo, who produces an ancient box containing three objects that might be the Grand Master's keys, and then from a police officer, Cortiñas, who turns out to have a vested interest in the dragon's well-being. When Hadrián goes missing, his mother calls the police, but only Mónica knows where he really is. Will she inform the police and break her promise not to reveal where he is hiding? If she does, will the police be in time to save her friend, and what will become of the dragon he has started to turn into?

ISBN 978-954-384-042-7